BACKWOODS
RIPPER

A gripping action suspense thriller

ANNA WILLETT

Paperback edition published by

The Book Folks

London, 2017

ISBN 978-1-5208-1616-6

www.thebookfolks.com

For my mother, Monica,
who taught me to love books.

Chapter One

Paige Loche turned the radio off and regarded her husband. With one lightly tanned arm draped over the wheel, and the other resting on his thigh, Hal looked completely relaxed. One of the things she loved about him was his stillness. Even with the birth of their first baby only two months away, he managed to remain calm and unfazed while Paige experienced a stab of panic every time she thought about what lay ahead.

"Tired of the music?" he asked, and shifted his hand to her leg.

"Just feeling a bit queasy."

They'd left the highway thirty minutes ago in search of a side road heading to the east of Mount Barker. At first the bushland on either side of the single lane road offered a welcome change from the bland and uneventful highway. But after watching the trees spin by for the last ten minutes, Paige felt her stomach churn and her lower back throb.

"I'll find a turn off and a clearing where we can pull over." Hal rubbed Paige's thigh while keeping an eye on the road.

"Thanks." She picked up his hand and turned it over so she could run her finger over the tattoo on the inside of his wrist. She could feel his pulse beating a steady rhythm beneath his warm skin. When they first met, Hal's tattoo unnerved her. But over time, the vicious red snake – weaving its way around a dagger – became one more thing about her husband she'd grown to love.

"Don't worry, after the baby comes, I'm getting it removed."

"Don't you dare." Paige lifted his wrist to her lips. "It's grown on me and … and it's part of who you are."

"I thought you hated it?" Hal laughed.

"Hate is a strong word." Paige put his hand on her belly. "Besides it can be a useful cautionary tale about what not to do when you're drunk." She felt the baby move. A long shifting sensation travelled across her stomach, as if sensing its father's touch. "Feel that?"

Hal gave her a sideways look over the top of his sunglasses and smiled: Hal, with his messy brown hair and two-day old stubble looking healthy and strong, as if he could take on the world.

* * *

"Spring Road. I don't remember seeing it on the map, but it might be privately owned," Hal said, and swung the car right. "With any luck there'll be a clearing where we can pull over."

The sign announcing Spring Road leaned dangerously close to the ground at a sixty-degree angle, almost as if pointing towards some hidden passage to the centre of the earth. On either side of the narrow road, thick scrub and ancient gum trees crowded the bitumen. Paige leaned back and shifted her butt until her back straightened. It had been two hours since they last took a break and she looked forward to stretching her back.

"Is that a house?" Paige motioned towards a clearing on the left.

Amidst the tightly-packed greenery, a dusty white building sat in a sea of cracked bitumen, now a home for sprigs of yellowing weeds. The building looked at odds with its surroundings, as if an industrial structure had dropped from a passing aeroplane and landed haphazardly in the midst of the bush.

"Whatever it is, I'd say it's abandoned now." Hal pulled the car off the road and onto the aging bitumen. Bits of stone and scattered twigs crackled under the wheels of the Ford EcoSport. "There's a bit of shade at the end of the building," he said and drove around the carpark.

The building comprised of two squat brick structures on either side of a tall, broad tower with a pointed tin roof. The façade had been rendered – at least fifty years ago – and painted white, now faded to a streaky water-stained grey. On the far left of the structure, the carpark dipped and a cluster of peppermint trees circled the crumbling edges of the property.

"Silver Island Cheese." Paige read the cursive black writing above the building's main door. "It's sort of creepy."

"It's a cheese factory; I don't think there's anything less creepy," Hal said with a chuckle, and turned the car in a slow arc to park under the shade of the trees. "Come on, we can sit on the loading bay."

For a moment Paige didn't move. She scanned the front of the building for signs of life. Something about the hulking structure seemed out of place in the isolated setting. She pinched her lower lip between her thumb and index finger.

"It's not like we're planning on breaking into the place." Hal sensed her trepidation. "You can stretch your legs and take a breather. I'll grab us something to eat out of the Esky. We'll have a picnic." He looked around. "I don't see any chainsaw-wielding maniacs so I think we'll be okay."

Paige rolled her eyes skyward. "Okay, but if I get chopped up, I'm blaming you," she said, suppressing a smile.

Hal grabbed a picnic rug and the cooler from the rear of the vehicle, and walked over to the loading dock. He spread the rug out near the edge and pulled a can of coke out of the Esky. Just watching him drink made Paige need to pee. She rubbed the small of her back and turned away. The bush on the far side of the car would do the trick, but the thought of squatting in the thick scrub while trying to balance her swollen belly was unappealing to say the least. Then there was the tiny matter of snakes. She shuddered and turned back to Hal.

"Do you want a drink?" he asked, holding up a bottle of water.

Paige's shoulders slumped. "I need to pee, but I'm worried about snakes in the bush."

Hal put his coke down and walked back towards her. "Just do it around the other side of the car. There's no one around, why go in the bush?"

Paige turned and looked at the road. They hadn't seen another car for at least twenty minutes. The baby gave a sudden kick and the pressure on her bladder intensified.

She sighed. "Okay. Why not?"

She took care positioning herself near the dip that lead to the peppermint trees so the urine would flow down and away from her feet. The relief felt almost erotic in its intensity. Paige let out a long breath and looked up. A magpie sat in the overhanging branch, its head cocked to one side; it fixed a black beady eye on her.

If the magpie decided to swoop at her, Paige would likely tumble backwards and land in her own pee. She grimaced and tried to force her bladder to empty, but it had been a long car ride and judging by the steady stream that chugged towards the peppermint trees, she wasn't slowing down any time soon. She cursed under her breath and clutched her knees.

4

"What did you say?"

"Nothing!" Paige winced at the shrillness of her voice and glanced back up at the magpie. It regarded her with blank intensity and rubbed its beak on the edge of the branch. *Getting it nice and sharp,* Paige thought grimly and watched the creature hop a little farther down the branch. She felt her stream start to dwindle and smiled. A second later, she pulled up her pants, gave the bird a smug look over her shoulder and walked back around the car.

"Feeling better?"

"You wouldn't belie-"

"Look out!" Hal's smile dropped and his mouth opened. He stepped towards her, arms up.

Paige started to ask what he meant when something grazed the right side of her head. There was no pain, just a jolt. In her periphery she saw a blur of black moving so quickly she could've imagined it. Stumbling forward, Paige almost lost her footing, but Hal reached her in time.

"I knew that thing was going to swoop at me."

"Are you okay?" He held her left elbow to steady her.

"Yes, I'm fine," Paige laughed. "Lucky I've got you to catch me." She looked up into his face and the smile died on her lips.

He'd drained of colour and his lips were tight. Pulling her closer, he encircled her in his arms. She leaned her head against his chest and listened to his heart beat; it sounded fast. Had her near-fall startled him so badly? She laced her arms around his back and felt his muscles warm and hard beneath his T-shirt.

* * *

Hal, a little over six foot with a large, muscular frame, had just left the army when Paige met him. He'd been working as a plumber – a trade learned in the armed forces. Strong, gentle, and lighthearted, but never glib; he made Paige feel safe.

"I'm sorry if I scared you." Paige pulled back from the hug, searching Hal's eyes.

He looked away; she could see a redness creep up his neck. She frowned.

"Hal? Is something wrong?"

He kissed her on top of the head, turned away, and walked towards the loading bay. "It's nearly three o'clock, we should get going." He folded the picnic blanket.

Paige could tell he was upset, maybe even embarrassed about something. It'd probably be best to just let it go and wait until he wanted to talk about it. But Hal never fretted about little things.

"Hal, tell me what's going on? You're worrying me." Paige put her hand on his elbow and turned him away from the Esky.

He put the rug down and faced her. "It's nothing, really."

Paige put her hands on her hips and cocked her head to the side. Hal gave a long sigh and said, "Okay, but it's nothing. I wouldn't even say anything, but I know you won't let it go until I do."

Paige wanted to ask what he meant by *won't let it go,* but held her tongue.

"When you came around from behind the car and the magpie swooped you." He paused and looked over her shoulder to where the car was parked. "I got a ..." He scratched his head and shrugged.

"You got a what?" Paige asked her voice dropping to a whisper.

"I don't know." He laughed, a dry nervous sound. "It's nothing. I just got a fright when you almost fell." Hal held her gaze. "I'm fussing, I know."

"No." Paige put her hand on Hal's arm. "You're not fussing. We're miles from the medical centre in Mount Barker, the last thing we want is an emergency out here." She looked around at the abandoned factory and the dense green bushland seeming to crowd closer with every passing minute. "I don't know if I'm just too much of a city girl,

6

but this place gives me the creeps. I say we go." She released Hal's arm and snatched up the picnic blanket.

Hal grabbed the Esky and followed his wife to the rear of the car. Loose gravel and bits of debris crunched under their shoes. The boot-space held their two suitcases, road snacks, and paper towels, supporting their plan to spend a few weeks exploring the South West before the baby arrived. A carefree "babymoon" seemed like the perfect way to transition from newlyweds to parents.

Paige watched Hal push the matching black cases aside and put the cooler into the back of the car. Their next stop, Mount Barker. The small town tourist spot allowed visitors to enjoy the fruits of the Great Southern wine region. *Not that I'll get the chance to sample the wine*, she thought. Hopefully the side trip to the crazy cheese factory wouldn't sour their last week on the road.

She tucked a stray strand of hair behind her ear and tossed the picnic rug on top of the Esky. "I don't like the look of those clouds." Paige nodded up at the sky to the previously blue expanse.

Hal followed her gaze and nodded. "They get some heavy rainfall down here, even in spring. But we'll be long gone before the downpour starts." Hal slammed the hatch closed and gave Paige a playful pat on the butt. "Let's go, Honey. I plan on getting us to Mount Barker by five, and placing a cold beer in my hand by six."

"You mean my swollen feet in your hands," Paige teased, pleased that Hal sounded upbeat.

Paige opened the passenger door and grabbed her denim jacket. The wind had kicked up and the temperature dipped. She slipped the jacket over her white cotton dress and slowly hoisted herself up onto the seat. She glanced across the driver's side and noticed Hal standing outside. He was looking down, a frown creasing his brow. *What now?*

Paige opened her mouth to ask what he was doing, but his head ducked out of sight. An icy sensation touched the back of her neck. She slid back out of the car and walked around to the driver's side. Hal crouched on the ground inspecting the tyre. Paige noticed a line of sweat gathering on the back of his neck.

"It's flat." Hal looked up and pointed to a gash in the tread.

For a moment their gazes locked. Something flickered in Hal's green eyes. It was only there for a fraction of a second, but Paige knew she'd seen it. If she didn't know better, she'd swear her husband looked scared.

The saliva in her mouth evaporated. She reminded herself that he'd been in far more dangerous situations during his time in the army. This was nothing more than a flat tyre. His anxiety probably stemmed from being stranded with a pregnant woman. *Who wouldn't be?* Her doctor had assured her the long car trip was perfectly safe as long as she took rest breaks. The worse that could happen would probably be fatigue and dizziness. Even so, she understood his anxiety.

Paige put her hand on her belly and bit her lower lip. Hal stood and gave the tyre one last kick before trekking around to the back of the car. He unloaded the suitcases and the Esky, working quickly, trying to get the tyre changed before the rain fell.

"This won't take long," Hal said, and bounced the spare out of its mount on the tailgate.

Paige nodded and managed a weak smile. She glanced back at the empty building. Three large windows faced the carpark, the glass looked black behind the wire mesh covering them. The windows higher up in the centre point of the tower were boarded over. Paige wondered what they were trying to keep out, *animals or people?* She pulled her jacket closed across her chest and shivered.

Hal balanced on one knee, working silently he jacked up the front of the vehicle and unscrewed the lug nuts. When he had the flat safely off the axle, Paige moved a little closer. In spite of the chill creeping into the air, a dark line of sweat marred the back of his T-shirt.

"Nearly done," he said and lifted the spare up to the bare rim.

"What do you think caused the flat?" The question nagged at her from the moment Hal showed her the gash in the tyre. The dilapidated carpark was covered in bits of gravel and twigs, but she couldn't see anything that would've torn a hole that large.

"It could have been a broken bottle or – holy shit!" Hal jumped back from the tyre. His right leg drawn up in pain. As he pushed himself away from the car, his left foot hit the jack out of position and the vehicle dropped suddenly. The spare fell out of his grasp and spun sideways.

A crack, like a branch snapping rang out and then the car bounced. Hal's head snapped back as he cried out. Paige shrieked and lunged forward hands outstretched.

"No!" He croaked and put up his hand to stop her approach.

She hesitated confused, then she saw the snake slither up near Hal's shoulder. He lay flat on his back holding his right leg up to his chest. His other leg still under the car next to the rim.

"Don't move," Paige gasped, keeping her eyes fixed on the shiny brown snake bobbing and weaving its way around her husband.

Her heart beat so hard it felt like it might come out of her mouth. She looked around for something to use as a weapon and spotted the tyre iron on Hal's far side. With the snake between her and the iron, Paige realised she'd have to make her way around the creature.

"I'm going to get the tyre iron," she whispered.

"No. No, Paige," Hal groaned. "Don't." He tried to move and his eyes widened; he gasped and lowered his head. The snake slithered closer to Hal, its slimy body undulating as its pale underbelly rasped over the bitumen.

"Shhh," Paige whispered and stepped to the side so she could move around his head and give the snake a wide berth.

Blood flooded Hal's face turning it from lightly tanned to almost purple. He was bathed in sweat and pain. Paige's eyes moved between Hal and the snake. She wanted to speak to him, tell him everything was going to be okay, but with each fraction she moved, the snake's head weaved between its hiding place next to Hal's head and Paige's feet. If she made a sound, it would strike.

She took another sidestep to the right. The snake lifted its blunt head, regarding her with blank, blackish-brown, reptilian eyes ringed with orange. Paige tried to swallow but couldn't. Hal's breath came heavy and raw.

"Don't move your head, it's right next to you," Paige whispered when Hal attempted to watch her progress. He didn't respond, but kept still.

Paige didn't know a great deal about snakes, but she did know that Western Australia was home to some of the world's most venomous. Snakes were one of the things that scared her when she and Hal made the move from Melbourne to Perth only six months ago. She remembered telling herself the fears were irrational. The chances of her ever coming face to face with a snake were slim to none. *Right.*

The thick-bodied creature coiled in front of her and darted its forked tongue out, tasting the air. Paige recalled reading that snakes were shy creatures, more scared of us than we were of them. It didn't look scared, in fact it looked supremely confident. Although it could be anything from mildly venomous to deadly, Paige knew she had to get it away from Hal before it struck again. And then there was that voice in the back of her head asking, *if it bites me, will it kill the baby?*

Paige felt beads of sweat run down the back of her neck. She resisted the urge to wipe them away and took another step. Now on Hal's right side, she noticed him following her progress from the corner of his eyes.

"Don't try and move it," he managed through clenched teeth. "Just go get your phone and call for help."

The sound of Hal's voice alarmed the snake. It moved with lightning speed, its sickly olive coloured body flicking up dried leaves and sticks as it darted for Hal's face. Paige stamped her foot and clapped her hands. The creature turned back towards her. She stooped and grabbed the tyre iron as the snake left Hal and lunged towards her, hissing. Its open mouth revealed small sharp fangs and the soft pink flesh within.

Paige screamed and tried to step back, but the creature lunged upwards as if about to take flight. An evil hissing filled her ears, blocking out all other sound. She crossed her left arm over her stomach hoping that the snake would bite the sleeve of her jacket and not her belly, but just as its head came within striking range, it jack-knifed backwards and landed on the ground with a thump.

It took Paige a split second to realise Hal had grabbed hold of the snake's tail. The creature wreathed and twisted in his hand, its head turning towards her husband's face, its jaws gaping at an impossibly wide angle. Using both hands, Paige swung the tyre iron over her shoulder and down, landing a shuddering blow on the creature's head. The iron crushed the snake into the bitumen, the impact sent a shock wave up Paige's right arm.

Lifting the tyre iron with shaking hands, she pounded the creature a second time. The first blow crushed the snake's skull, the second almost separated its head from its long thick body.

"Are you okay?" Hal's voice sounded distant.

Paige looked past the crushed snake and found her husband's eyes. Unshed tears glistening on his lower lids. She nodded stiffly. He'd turned onto his right side, still gripping the snake's tail.

Paige used the end of the tyre iron to flick the reptile's lifeless body away from Hal. She stepped closer and sank to her knees, ignoring the roughness of the broken bitumen under her skin, she leaned down and put her head on his chest. She felt his hand grip the back of her head and hold her against him. For a moment the only sounds were Hal's breathing and her sobs.

"Are you bitten?" she asked cupping his face with her hands.

"Yeah. It got me on the calf. But it's my other leg." Hal grimaced and tried to sit up. He got as far as his elbows on the ground and stopped moving. "When I hit the jack out, the rim hit it when the car bounced down. I think it's broken."

"Don't try and move." She put her hand on his chest. "I'm going to call an ambulance." Paige stripped off her jacket and tucked it under his head. "I'll be right back, okay?" She waited for Hal to nod and then gave him a kiss on the mouth. His lips were icy.

Rising, she jogged around the car. The passenger door stood open; her handbag sat on the floor. She grabbed her phone. She'd only ever called an ambulance once before, the day her father died. He'd had a heart attack during the night. Paige remembered opening his bedroom door, it was after eight in the morning, but his blinds were still closed. The air in the room tasted hot and stale. At first she'd thought he was asleep. The sheets were all rumpled; they looked grey in the thin bars of light seeping through the blinds. She'd called to him, but he hadn't responded. She'd put her hand out and touched the top of the dresser near the door. Something landed on it. Something black and thick, and she could feel its legs moving on her skin. She flicked her hand and the fly had buzzed up to her face.

Paige closed her eyes and forced away the memory. *Hal isn't going to die.* His youth and strength reassured her this time she wouldn't be too late. She tried to slide the bar across the screen to unlock her phone, but her hands shook badly, she could barely make her fingers work. When she finally got the phone open, a *no signal* warning flashed at the top left of the screen.

"No. No." She shook her head and brought up the keypad, refusing to believe they were cut off.

She dialled triple zero and pressed the phone to her ear muttering a prayer. For a couple of seconds nothing happened, then a series of beeps. Paige squeezed her eyes closed and shook the phone. She looked around as if hoping to find herself on a busy street, instead of stranded in front of a crumbling factory in the middle of nowhere. Her eyes blurred with tears and her breathing came in rapid gasps. She struggled to breathe past the panic filling her throat.

She had to act. She took a long, deep breath and jogged back around the car. A black crow sat a few metres away trying to pick up the snake's carcass in its long black beak. Another crow pecked at the snake's head, snatching up bits of decimated meat off the bitumen. The birds paused in their work as she approached. The crow, picking at the head, let out a squawk and Hal's eyes flew open. He looked pale and his teeth chattered.

"Oh God, Hal. You're freezing." Paige knelt next to him.

She put her hand on his face, his skin icy to the touch. His eyes fluttered and then closed, but the shivering continued. *He's going into shock*; the realisation got her moving. She raced to the rear of the car, baby bump swaying, and grabbed the picnic rug; she then returned and draped it over her husband.

She knelt down and tucked the blanket around him. His left leg was bent slightly. Paige saw the snake bite just above his ankle. The area looked puffy; two red fang marks surrounded by purplish skin. His other leg remained under the car, his calf concealed by the vehicle.

"Hal?" She whispered. "Hal, I don't have a signal on my phone. I ... What should I do?" She hated the whiny sound of her voice. Hal needed her. He needed her to take charge for once and be the strong one.

Hal's eyes opened. "Send a text, it will work with a lower signal." He sounded groggy, like someone waking from a dream.

Paige let out a whimper of relief and fumbled with her phone. She typed a message and pressed *send*. The message bar moved slowly, crawling its way across the screen, then stopped. She stared at the phone and tucked her lower lip under her teeth.

"Hal, it's not working. I'm going to have to go for help," she said. "I ... Will you be ..."

Hal pulled his arm from under the rug and grabbed her hand. "I'll be fine," he said. "It's just a broken leg." He tried for a smile, but it looked more like a grimace.

Chapter Two

Paige strode as fast her aching back would allow. She headed back along Spring Road in the direction they'd taken after leaving the highway. From there, she planned to backtrack the ten or so kilometres it would take to reach the Albany Highway. With any luck, someone would drive past before she got that far.

She walked on the road rather than risk turning an ankle on the shoulder, trying to keep left, and concentrated on taking even breaths every two steps. She checked her watch; three-forty. The snake bit Hal just after three. She wondered, not for the first time, how long it would be before the venom spread and became fatal. She knew one thing for sure, he needed medical help, now.

Paige increased her pace, wishing she could break into a run. After leaving the cheese factory, she tried wrapping both arms around her belly for support while running. Within minutes, her heart pounded as her legs hit the underside of her stomach, making her woozy. The breeze blew up crisp and carried a chill, but the pace she'd set for herself kept her warm.

The only sounds came from the constant beat of her canvas shoes, her steady breathing, and the rustling of the trees and shrubs as the wind whispered through their branches. Overhead, the sky darkened with murky clouds. She tried to ignore the dimness creeping in and kept her mind from imagining what it would be like to spend a night surrounded by thick twisted trees shrouded in spider webs. She focused on the road, scanning the horizon for oncoming cars and occasionally looking back in case someone approached from the other direction. Her mind kept returning to Hal: the ashen colour of his skin and the clammy feel of his hand when she tucked it back under the picnic rug and kissed him goodbye. *Goodbye. Was it goodbye?* Would he be gone when she got back? Paige didn't know where the irrational thought kept coming from, but out here, amidst a wildness that didn't exist in her world of cafes and yoga classes, anything might be lurking. In a place where snakes hid under your car and birds fought over their carcases; her worst fears seemed possible.

She glanced at the tightly-packed trees and ragged scrub lining the road, wondering what lurked just out of sight. She hugged herself and felt the goose flesh. Spots of cold rain hit her shoulders. She thought of Hal semi-conscious as the rain attacked his unprotected head. Paige could only hope he'd be able to pull the rug up to shield himself.

She reached under her bra strap, pulled out her phone and checked for a signal. Still nothing. *This is the South West, not the Gibson Desert.* Paige let out a long, shaky sigh and stopped walking. She wiped sporadic rain drops from her cheeks and turned in a circle. The sky, heavy with dark threatening clouds blocked the sun and cast a shroud over the landscape.

Paige turned back in the direction of the highway and blinked away the drops that ran down her forehead and clung to her eyelashes. She heard the ute before she saw the glow of its lights: a reverberating rumble, low, barely audible above the sound of the rain. At first, she thought the sound came from her chest, until it grew louder and twin orbs of light filled the road.

"Stop!" she called, her voice barely louder than a croak.

Stepping into the middle of the road, she waved her arms above her head. "Stop! Please, help!"

The bull bar and the silver grille glistened between the yellowy glow of the headlights as the engine shuddered with a roar of vintage engineering. Paige's heart fluttered and her arms shook as she held them out in front of her like white sticks. The vehicle would have to stop or swerve around her, but she wouldn't move.

A horn blasted, shrill and urgent, tyres squealed. Paige gasped out a heavy breath and flinched as the ute came to a stop a metre from her outstretched arms. She wiped her arm across her face and squinted at the windscreen. Beyond the blur of the wipers, she caught the shadowy outline of two people.

Her stomach clenched and the relief she'd felt only seconds ago was swallowed by fear. *I'm all alone. They could be dangerous.* She felt her muscles tighten, the urge to run building inside her until the driver's door swung open with a metallic groan and a woman stepped out into the rain.

"Oh Lord, what's happened! Have you been in an accident?" she asked, her eyes wide.

Paige let out a shuddering breath and stumbled forward. "Yes. Yes, I need help." She struggled to find the right words.

The woman looked around and frowned. Paige realised she was looking for a wrecked car.

"At the cheese factory. My husband. He... Snake bite." She took a step closer to the woman, desperate that she understand, but fearful she'd frighten the woman back into her car.

"My husband is hurt and I need help." Paige tried again, but her words were coming out as breathless gasps.

She resisted the urge to grab the woman's arm and shake her. Instead, she pressed her lips together and waited.

The woman looked to be in her late fifties, stocky with iron grey hair. She looked Paige over as if assessing her for a job. Her eyes paused on Paige's belly and then she nodded.

"Okay. Well, you'd better get in," she said and jerked her thumb in the direction of the ute. "I know the place you mean; the old Silver Island factory."

"Yes, that's it. That's the place." Paige wanted to fall into the woman's arms and kiss her, but something in the woman's demeanour told her it wouldn't be wise.

"Hurry up," she said, turning and walking back to the open door of the vehicle. "Let's get out of the rain."

Paige scampered after the woman, shivering and rubbing her arms against the chill of the rain. When they reached the door, the woman stood back and motioned Paige into the cab. Paige grabbed the seat and moved forward to pull herself into the vehicle when she noticed the other occupant.

On the far side of the cab sat a large woman with short black hair, a blank stare and protruding bottom lip. Paige hesitated. She felt the hairs on the back of her neck rise and, for a moment, she considered backing away. She could keep walking, someone else was bound to come along.

"Come on. I'm getting soaked out here," the other woman called from behind her.

Paige pushed her fear aside, muttered a hello to the woman in the cab and climbed in.

The inside of the old ute smelled like aged vinyl. Paige could feel the bulge of springs under her butt. She sat packed in between the two women, their collective breath fogging the windows, as the gear stick wedged awkwardly between her legs.

"My name's Lizzy. Lizzy Hatcher and that's Soona," she said, and motioned to the dark-haired woman on Paige's right.

"I'm Paige Loche." She felt like she needed to add something so she said, "Thank you for stopping, Lizzy."

"You're lucky we found you," Lizzy said grinding the ancient gearstick. "This road is unincorporated so we're the only ones who use it."

The engine rumbled, then sputtered, missing a few revs before evening out. There were no seatbelts so Paige gripped the edge of the seat. The rain continued to fall in large spits, rather than a full downpour. She pictured Hal laying half under the car waiting for her to return, his face ashen with pain as the poison worked its way through his body. She looked at her watch: four o'clock. Almost an hour now. She clenched the seat tighter, bouncing over every pothole and bump in the road. In spite of the discomfort, she wished Lizzy would drive faster.

"How far is it to the nearest town?"

"Two hours to the roadhouse," Lizzie answered, without taking her eyes off the road. "What sort of snake?"

"What?"

"What sort of snake bit your husband," Lizzy asked slowly, emphasising each word as if talking to a child.

Paige wasn't sure how to answer. Her knowledge of snakes only went as far knowing that some were deadly, but all were slimy and terrifying. The snake that attacked Hal seemed aggressive. In her mind's eye, she could see the moment the creature lunged at her. Its jaws wide, fleshy pink mouth reaching for her. If Hal hadn't grabbed it when he did, they might both be lying next to the car.

Paige shivered. "I don't know."

"Well, what did it look like?" Lizzy persisted.

Paige tried to visualise the snake. "It had a thick brown body, and head. Sort of lighter than the rest of it. I mean the head was lighter than the body." Paige watched Lizzy's profile as she described the snake. Her face remained impassive.

"Sounds like a dugite."

Paige let out a gasp and let go of the seat. The car hit a pothole and she bounced up almost a quarter of a metre. One thing she did know, dugites were highly venomous.

"Don't worry, I'm a trained nurse. I've treated snake bites before. The key is compression. What time was he bitten?"

"About an hour ago." Paige ran her fingers through her damp hair and tried to explain what happened. She finished by telling the woman about not being able to get a signal. Lizzy listened without interruption, nodding occasionally but not taking her eyes from the road. Paige glanced over at Soona. The woman had yet to speak but seemed to be fascinated by Paige's belly, unapologetically staring.

"Well, we'll soon find out what shape he's in," Lizzy said flatly and nodded to the road ahead. "There's the factory."

Paige leaned forward, holding her breath. Hal was her whole world. Before she'd met him, she'd lived an empty life, drifting. Yes, she had her job and she enjoyed teaching, but it didn't anchor her to the world the way Hal managed to. When they'd first met, he'd just started his new job.

One day she'd arrived home to find she had no hot water. Frustrated and in desperate need of a bath, she flicked through the local paper and found an ad for a plumbing service. Three hours later, Hal appeared in her life: tall, good looking, and easy to talk to. Just his presence in her house breathed life into the place. She recalled the way she'd blushed while explaining about the hot water.

Paige shook off the memory only to have it replaced by the image of her husband lying under the car, watching her walk away. His fate, tied up in hers, was out of their hands.

Lizzy pulled into the carpark and stopped behind the Ford. Paige could see the front of their car, but Hal remained hidden from view. Lizzy opened the driver's door and climbed out, at a pace that to Paige felt painful in its slowness. As soon as the woman stepped out of the cab, Paige scampered out behind her. When her shoes hit the bitumen, Paige dodged around the woman and darted to the Ford.

"Paige?" She heard his weakened voice before she saw him. Her pulse, already racing, jacked up another notch.

He lay next to the car. A pair of magpies danced on the loading dock watching him with emotionless eyes. It looked like he'd tried to pull himself out from under the vehicle, but had only made it a half-metre or so. The blanket lay bunched around his waist and his T-shirt looked damp, either from sweat or the rain. Paige sank down next to him and ran her palm over his face then took his hand.

"It's okay, Hal. I've brought help. You'll be alright now," she said, trying to reassure him and herself.

"Are you okay?" he asked breathlessly.

Paige nodded. "I am now I'm looking at you."

He was still conscious, a good sign, she hoped, but his skin was the colour of ashes and his eyes were wet and ringed with red.

"Are you in a lot of pain?" she asked, studying his face.

"Right. I'm going to need something I can use as bandages and something for a splint," Lizzy said from behind her, cutting off whatever Hal had been about to say.

Paige held Hal's gaze. For a fleeting moment, she felt outside of herself. An unshakable sense that she might lose him swept over her.

"Now, Paige," Lizzy snapped. "We need to work fast."

Paige reluctantly let go of Hal's hand and stood. She felt the blood rushing to her head and a wave of dizziness. She dropped her head and leaned on the Ford for balance.

After a pause, she looked up and Lizzy and Soona were on the ground with her husband.

"Hurry up and find me something I can use as a pressure bandage on this bite," Lizzy ordered.

Paige pushed herself off the vehicle and stumbled around to the passenger side of the Ford. *The first aid kit's in the glove box.* She pulled it open and grabbed the red nylon case before racing back around the bonnet.

"Okay. Good. Now find something I can use as a splint. Two lengths about a metre long and rigid." She spoke over her shoulder and unzipped the first aid case.

Paige put a hand to the side of her head. She tried to go through the contents of the boot in her mind, but could think of nothing that fit Lizzy's requirements. She turned in a circle, biting her lip, when she noticed the gum trees across the road. She remembered teaching her year two pupils about gum trees and how they shed branches so they could retain the moisture within the rest of the tree to survive.

She jogged out of the carpark and across the deserted road; the rain had finally stopped. The area under the trees remained draped in shadows and littered on the ground were fallen sticks and gum nuts. She scanned the area for something larger, but in her panic, everything blurred into a confusing jumble. She forced herself to slow down. She was no good to Hal running around blindly.

Paige closed her eyes and counted to five. When she opened them, she saw a metre-long stick as thick as her wrist, nestled amongst the fallen leaves. She let out a cry of triumph and snatched it up. Within a few seconds, she had another with suitable proportions and headed back to the Ford.

Halfway across the road Paige faltered when a cry broke the silence. A deep ragged sound of pain that echoed off the road and drove birds from the safety of the trees. She staggered, then broke into a run. Skidding across the carpark she became aware of the birds fluttering overhead and the sound of voices in hurried conversation.

She reached the Ford and found Lizzy and Soona crouched over Hal. His teeth were gritted in pain and a sheen of sweat covered his face.

"What are you doing to him?" Paige demanded, pushing Soona away from her husband.

"Calm down." Lizzy's voice lashed her like a whip crack.

Paige turned to face the woman. She could feel the anger building inside her. "Calm down? Why was he screaming?" She locked eyes with Lizzy. "What were you doing?"

Lizzy's eyes were a blue so pale they looked like bulbous chips of ice staring out of her square face. She drew her eyebrows together and clamped her lips into a thin line.

"We pulled him out from under the car so I could examine his injured leg," she said, clearly not used to being questioned. "But if you don't want our help …" She let her words hang in the air.

Angry red blotches blossomed on Lizzy's cheeks. Paige wanted to push her and the other woman away from her husband. A feeling deep in her gut told her that Hal needed protecting, but from what, Paige wasn't sure.

Lizzy shrugged and stepped back. "Right. We'll leave you to it," she said and jerked her head at Soona.

"No. No, I'm sorry," Paige stuttered. "Please. I just …" She grasped Lizzy's arm and the women recoiled from her.

Shocked, Paige dropped her hands to her side and tried again. "Lizzy, I'm sorry. I over-reacted. We do want your help. Please." Paige stopped talking and waited while Lizzy stood there thinking. As well as anger, Paige saw a momentary flicker of pleasure in the woman's eyes. The look appeared and vanished so quickly, Paige wondered if she even saw it. *Could Lizzy enjoy having so much power over her?*

"When I heard Hal cry out, I just …" Paige put her hand on her belly, hating herself for playing the pregnancy card. "I'm a bit emotional."

Lizzy looked from Paige's face to her belly then nodded. Paige let out a breath and swallowed hard. If it had been anyone else, Paige didn't think she'd have any problem with asking for help. Begging Lizzy left a sour taste in her mouth, but she had no option, except to placate the women until they got Hal to a hospital.

"I see you found something," Lizzy said pointing at the sticks in Paige's other hand.

Paige nodded, relieved the woman's anger had dissipated. Lizzy nodded to Soona, and the big woman took the sticks from Paige's hands.

Paige looked down at Hal. His eyes were closed, but his breathing sounded even. She noticed that the snake bite had been bandaged and felt a pang of regret for judging Lizzy so harshly. They'd obviously been administering first aid. Her eyes drifted to Hal's left leg and she sucked in her breath.

His lower leg was swollen to at least twice its normal size. Just above his ankle she saw a gash deep enough to expose muscle and bone. Paige put her hand over her mouth to block the gasp that threatened to escape. She began to lower herself next to her husband when Lizzy's arm shot out in front of her.

"No," she ordered. "You need to move back and let us do what we need to do."

Confused, Paige looked from the sticks in Soona's hands to the crooked angle of Hal's ankle, realisation dawned on her. They meant to straighten and splint his leg. She shook her head and started to protest, but Lizzy grabbed her shoulders and turned her away.

"You wanted our help," she reminded Paige. "We can't get him in the ute unless we splint his leg."

"But the pain," Paige moaned, and felt like the world had turned upside down. It seemed like only moments ago that she and Hal were laughing and making plans for the future. The next instant she found herself handing him over to two strange women, agreeing to let them hurt him in unimaginable ways. Her legs felt weak and her mouth suddenly dry.

She walked on numb legs and stood behind the old Holden. Bitterly aware of her own cowardice, she crouched down and covered her ears. When the screaming shredded the air, she closed her eyes and whispered "sorry" over and over. The horror of that moment eclipsed everything that had gone before in Paige's life.

Chapter Three

The shadows grew long across the bitumen as evening rushed to block out the day. Paige sat in the bed of the old Holden, one hand on Hal's chest to feel its constant rise and fall, the other gripping the side of the tray. His eyes stayed closed and he slept. She brushed back a lock of brown hair from his damp forehead.

After Lizzy and Soona had finished splinting Hal's leg, he'd lapsed into unconsciousness. "Shock" was Lizzy's one-word explanation for his condition.

He stirred again when the three women eased him onto an old door which Soona found around the back of the factory, and lifted him onto the back of the ute. As the door landed on the bed of the Holden, Hal's eyes had opened and he'd groaned before slipping back into unconsciousness.

Paige dragged her eyes away from her husband and watched the road disappearing in front of her. On either side, lush bushes and shrubs turned from green to grey in the dusky light. At irregular intervals, towering gum trees lined the road. Paige stared blankly around seeing only isolation. Lizzy had convinced her that the two-hour drive to the nearest roadhouse would put Hal at further risk. It made sense that a twenty-minute drive to Lizzy's house to use the phone would be safer than driving Hal over rough roads for two hours. So, instead of speeding towards civilisation, they were heading farther away.

Paige's back throbbed and her butt felt raw from sitting on the worn rubber mat lining the ute's tray. With each bounce and dip, her discomfort intensified. She hated herself for even acknowledging her own distress when Hal suffered so much. *I'm weak and a coward. I should've held his hand, but I was scared.* She thought of the way she'd hidden, her face burning with shame.

She wondered if she was doing the right thing by agreeing to go back to Lizzy's instead of the roadhouse. Was she doing it because she was too weak to argue and too tired to fight for her husband? She hoped Hal wouldn't pay the price for her feebleness. She pulled her phone out of her bra and checked the time; five-fifteen. They'd been driving for fifteen minutes.

Less than five minutes later, the ute veered to the left and Paige felt it make a wide arc. She turned and peered through the back window of the cab, but grime and dust blocked her view. She took her hand off Hal's chest and leaned over the tray, drawing up her knees and swivelling her head to lean over and see the front of the vehicle, like a refugee scouring the coast for a safe harbour.

The house took her breath away, and for a moment, her mouth hung open in disbelief. She'd expected a modest country cottage, not the sprawling three storey ornate Edwardian mansion that loomed out of the hill like a tombstone. Nothing about Lizzy and Soona gelled with the house. Their clothes were clean, but well-worn, and their vehicle ancient and on its last legs. How then, Paige wondered, did they come to live in a mansion?

As they drew closer, Paige noticed the crumbling brickwork and the sagging roof. Even in the dying light, she could see the building needed an overhaul. Even so, the place was a monster and the thought of Lizzy and

Soona rattling around in it, out here in the middle of nowhere, seemed more than a little eerie.

The Holden came to a stop to the right of the building, where the wrap-around veranda turned the corner of the house and a ramp rose towards the back. Paige wanted to tell Hal that they'd arrived and soon she'd be phoning for help, but he seemed peaceful and blessedly pain free so she decided not to disturb him.

The doors of the cab flung open on both sides and Lizzy and Soona clambered out.

"Go get one of the stretchers," Lizzy said.

Soona nodded and lumbered towards the front of the house, her faded denim dungarees bunched up between her long sloping butt cheeks.

"Maybe we should leave him here," Paige said over the side of the tray. "Getting him out of the ute will be painful, why don't we leave it for the paramedics?"

Lizzy watched Soona disappear around the house and then walked to the back of the Holden. She unbolted the flap and dropped it down. Paige crawled towards the woman on her hands and knees, careful to avoid bumping Hal as she went.

"I don't think we should move him," Paige said from the tray of the ute. "It's too painful."

Lizzy had to look up to meet Paige's eyes. The woman's mouth thinned to a straight line and her tangled grey brows drew together in determination. Paige swallowed and continued. "If you'll just watch him while I go inside and phone for help," she paused and forced out a dry laugh. "We'll be out of your hair soon."

Lizzy held her gaze for a second, Paige steeled herself for an argument. To her surprise, Lizzy nodded.

"The phone's in the kitchen. It's quicker to go around the back and up the stairs. Door's never locked," she said and stepped aside so Paige could climb down.

The area on the side of the house had probably once been lawn, now only a shambling expanse knee-high with weeds. She followed a path of broken flag stones that led away from the ramp and around the back of the building. The light disappeared fast, making each step a little more shadowed than the last. Paige picked her way along the path and had a crazy thought, *what if I fall and break my ankle? We'd be stuck here for God knows how long.* An irrational thought, but Paige slowed her pace and took care to put one tentative foot in front of another.

At the back of the house, the path met a set of rickety steps. A steep narrow climb on ancient greying wood led to the rear veranda and a once white screen door. On the left were tubs and cartons piled haphazardly. Some contained household goods including battered lamps and broken crockery. Others were overflowing with papers and books. A cluster of wicker chairs and a circular table sat on the right of a screen door. Farther to the right stood a rough stone wall and low archway that Paige guessed housed a laundry room. The whole area smelled of boiled vegetables and something sharp and chemical.

Paige opened the screen door and entered the kitchen. Enough weak light filtered in from the veranda to illuminate the details of her surroundings. A huge, heavy oak table dominated the room. Every inch of the place looked original, right down to the deep, speckled-concrete double sink.

Paige found a light switch on the far wall and flicked it on. The switch moved with a solid click and a single overhead bulb flickered to life. She looked around the room and spotted a grey rotary-style phone sitting on an ornate phone table complete with yellow velvet seat and cushioned armrest.

She tilted her head back and looked at the time-stained ceiling. She glanced over at the deep alcove housing a large, battered, iron stove, above it a mantle cluttered with old clocks and photos. On the wall above the mantle hung a framed needlepoint with the message; THE HEART OF HEAVEN IS THE HOME. She let out a long, even breath and blinked back tears. Until she'd seen the phone with her own eyes, there'd been a small frightened voice inside her – one that came from too many horror films – that didn't believe Lizzy and Soona had a phone.

She gave a little laugh and crossed the room. When Hal recovered, she'd tell him all about Lizzy and Soona. He'd see the funny side in all this and they'd look back on today and, well, maybe they wouldn't laugh, but at least find some dark humour in the situation.

Paige snatched up the receiver and dialled triple zero. The last zero spun back into place while she waited. A hollow emptiness on the line sent a cold finger down her spine. She squeezed her hand around the receiver and counted to three. Nothing. She clicked the slots up and down on the cradle and listened for a dial tone.

Silence.

She slammed down the receiver and grabbed the cord. It snaked out of the phone and into the wall. She pulled the cord out and then plugged it back in, hoping that securing it firmly in place would fix the problem. She lifted the receiver and listened. Nothing.

Paige sank down onto the velvet phone-seat and put her head in her hands. She felt like a mouse trapped in a maze of dead ends, desperate to escape but too stupid to stop scurrying around and think.

She ran her hands through her hair and then straightened up. She had no choice but to put her faith in Lizzy. The woman claimed to be a trained nurse, so maybe it was time to put her dislike for Lizzy aside and start thinking about what Hal needed. She stood and walked out of the kitchen.

"Your phone doesn't work," she said, approaching the ute. She hoped it didn't come out sounding as much like an accusation as it did in her head.

Lizzy and Soona stood on either side of a medical stretcher with folding legs and wheels, the sort used by ambulances to move patients, except this version looked larger and about twenty years out of date.

"I've had Comm Tec out twice this year, but it's always something. Water in the transfer box or dust on the overhead line." She shook her head. "Two women on their own should take priority, but do you think those big-wigs in the city care about people like us?" Lizzy asked, looking from Soona to Paige.

Soona ignored Lizzy and let her blank gaze settle on Paige's belly. Lizzy seemed to be waiting for someone to answer her so Paige asked, "How do we get help? If the phone's not working, what should we do?"

"We get him inside," she jerked her head towards Hal. "Then we get some fluids into him and monitor that bite until tomorrow. Once we've taken care of him, I'll drive to the roadhouse and get help." She paused and fixed Paige with her thin-lipped stare. "Unless you've got a better idea?"

"I'm all out of ideas."

Chapter Four

The accordion door stood open on the tarnished green, metal lift that dominated much of the black and white tiled foyer. The wheels on the trolley squealed with each rotation. Soona pushed the stretcher into the unlit lift; Lizzy crouched slightly and slammed the sliding gate.

"Take the stairs," Lizzy said and set the lift in motion.

Paige watched open-mouthed as the prehistoric lift creaked its way upwards and the two women's legs disappeared from sight. She climbed the wide staircase, shoes pounding on the faded blue runner, keeping time with the sluggish rise of the lift. It came to a wheezing halt on the third floor. Paige rounded the banister and watched Lizzy exit the lift and stride across the landing followed by Soona, pushing the stretcher.

Hal's eyes were open. He raised his head and looked at his wife. "Paige, where are we?" His words were slurred.

Paige reached out to take his hand, but Soona pushed the stretcher forward knocking her hand away. Paige fell in line behind the woman, but could see nothing bar Soona's wide back and bow-shaped rear end. She followed the women into a small narrow room. A single metal framed bed, stripped down to a bare mattress, stood against the wall.

"Get some sheets and make up the bed," Lizzy instructed, and then opened a narrow cupboard, its contents hidden by a panelled door. Soona let go of the stretcher and disappeared out of the room, her brown lace-up shoes, sliding across the hardwood floor.

Paige stepped up to the stretcher and took Hal's hand. "How do you feel?" She whispered, grateful to be looking into his eyes and speaking to him again.

"Like a car landed on me," he said.

Paige managed a weak smile and bent to kiss him on the forehead. His skin, cold before, now felt hot against her lips.

"I'm going to put in a bung and start you on a drip," Lizzy said in a terse tone. She wheeled a small trolley towards the stretcher. "It's important that we keep you hydrated. I'm also going to give you something for the pain, but nothing too strong," she added, as though Hal had said, "Give me the strong stuff."

"Is this a hospital?" Hal asked, frowning at his surroundings.

"This," said Lizzy with a grand sweep of her arm. "Is Mable House. It has been many things since it was built in 1928, but mostly a hospital." Her face glowed with excitement.

She picked up a surprisingly modern looking package from the trolley and tore it open. "Once I've sedated you, we'll get you settled in bed." She pulled a syringe from the packet and began drawing something from a small plastic bottle.

"Wait a minute," Hal said, his voice taking on a little more strength. He sat up on his elbows and tried to jerk away from the needle. His leg moved slightly to the right and he fell back onto the stretcher groaning and reaching for his injured limb.

33

Paige moved around Hal and positioned herself between Lizzy and her husband. "What are you giving him?" Lizzy looked like she knew what she was doing, but how much did they really know about her qualifications?

"It's a mild sedative," Lizzy said and pursed her lips. "If he doesn't have it, it'll hurt like buggery when we move him." She held the syringe pointed skyward.

Paige turned back to Hal. "It might help with the pain."

Hal nodded so Paige stepped aside and watched Lizzy slide the point of the needle into his arm.

Once Hal was settled in the bed, Paige stood next to him and put her hand on his. His eyes opened and he rolled his head towards her. "What did the doctor say?" he asked dreamily.

"You'll be fine. And tomorrow, we'll move you to another place."

His eyes closed, then opened again. "I love you," he said.

"I love you too," she whispered.

* * *

Paige bit into the cheese sandwich and forced her mouth to chew. The cheese was creamy and the bread soft and fluffy, but her mouth felt dry and the texture somehow gooey and sickening. She forced herself to swallow and take another mouthful. Soona nodded her approval and demolished her own sandwich in three large bites, chewing noisily and spraying crumbs onto the bib of her dungarees.

Paige focused on her plate and swallowed another clump of cheesy dough. She'd been inside the house for a little over an hour and, in spite of its enormity, the air felt stale and thick with dust. She put the remaining half of her sandwich down and took a sip of water.

"Thank you, Soona. That was nice, but I'm full," she said and patted her stomach.

Soona's eyes skipped between Paige's belly and her half-eaten sandwich.

"Would you like the rest?" Paige asked pushing her plate forward.

Soona managed to reach across the table and grab the sandwich without making eye contact. When her hand closed over the bread, Paige noticed the woman's arm: thick, muscular, and covered in dark hair. So far, she'd not heard Soona speak one word, but she obviously understood.

"Have you lived here long?" Paige asked.

Soona munched on the bread, eyes fixed on the scarred tabletop, but didn't respond.

Paige sighed and scratched her head. She should be grateful to Lizzy for helping Hal, but nothing about the woman or the house sat right. She wanted to believe that bringing Hal here had been the right decision, but couldn't ignore the strangeness of the situation. Even that, the decision, hadn't really been hers. At every turn, fate had conspired to deliver her to Mable House. *A hospital*, Lizzy said, but for what? There didn't seem to be anyone else in the building. The place seemed abandoned.

Paige checked the clock over the stove. Half an hour ago Lizzy had told her to go downstairs and have something to eat. She had to believe that bringing Hal here was the right decision. The only decision under the circumstances.

Paige fingered the wedding ring on her left hand. She'd had to remove her engagement ring last month because her fingers swelled, but had continued wearing her wedding ring even though it became painfully tight.

Soona pushed her chair back and picked up the dishes. She shambled over to the sink and ran the water. Paige looked towards the door to the drawing room, and wondered if Soona would try to stop her if she went upstairs. A crazy thought. No one wanted to stop her, *did they?* No, she couldn't let her thoughts run away with her.

The two women were oddballs, but they were genuinely trying to help.

"I think I'll go back up and see how Hal's doing," she said and stood up.

"He's doing very well," Lizzy said from the doorway. "He's sleeping."

"Okay. Good. I'll just sit with him," Paige said, and waited for Lizzy to clear the doorway.

Lizzy stood her ground, her shapeless body filling the exit. "I want a quick word with you," she said, and nodded to the chair Paige had just left.

Paige bit her lip and forced herself to calm down. She had no choice but to listen to what Lizzy had to say; to trust her. Paige sat.

Lizzy walked around the table and sat facing Paige. She placed her hands on the wooden surface and clenched them together. "The good news is that I think it may have been a dry bite."

Paige opened her mouth to ask what she meant, but Lizzy continued on. "That means he was bitten …" she paused. "But there was no venom."

"That's good," Paige said in a rush. "If there's no venom, he'll be okay and we can move him, right?"

Lizzy let out a long sigh. It was an impatient sound. "I said," her voice increased in volume. "I think it *may* have been a dry bite. Now, the only way I'll know for sure is if I monitor him all night. I daren't take the pressure bandage off because if there is venom, it'll spread like lightening and, bamb!" She pounded her fist making the table rattle and Paige flinch. "We'll lose him."

"Oh God," Paige said and put her hand to her chest.

"Now for the bad news," she continued. "His left leg is broken. The laceration is deep and I'm concerned about infection."

Paige felt her whole body slump. "I think we should drive into town right now and get help."

Lizzy's eyes narrowed to slits. "You listen here, Ducky," she said through a mouth so tight it resembled a duck's asshole. "I'm not moving him until I know there's no chance of the venom spreading. You wanted my help so we do this my way."

"We don't have to move him. He can stay here and we can drive into town," Paige said, her voice rising. "I don't know why we're just sitting here like idiots. Let's go?"

"I don't like your tone," Lizzy said.

"I'm sorry," Paige said, trying to get herself under control. "I just think that we need to get help. We should have just driven him into town in the first place."

Lizzy rolled her shoulders back and fixed her pale eyes on Paige. "If I leave him and he has a seizure or stops breathing, do you think Soona will be able to help him?"

Soona turned away from the sink and laughed. A humourless braying filled the room. It was the first time the woman had made a sound other than heavy breathing or chewing. Her eyes looked glassy and her mouth stretched into a frozen grin. Paige had seen similar expressions on the faces of autistic children she'd taught during her time as a junior school teacher. On children, the behaviour was innocent and symptomatic of the shut-off nature of autism, but on a large woman like Soona, the laugh and smile sent cold fingers of dread through Paige's chest.

"Okay. Okay," Paige said. "What about if Soona and I go into town?" She didn't like the idea of being alone in the car for two hours with Soona, but realised that she was running out of options.

Lizzy shook her head and made a clicking sound with her tongue.

"Why not?' Paige asked, her voice rising another notch.

"Because," Lizzy said. Soona can't drive. Can you drive a manual?" Something flickered in the woman's eyes.

Again, the look appeared for an instant and then skittered away.

Paige felt the air go out of her lungs. She wanted to argue, but she'd run out of suggestions. Lizzy was right, but her dislike for the woman boiled in her stomach like a bad case of reflux.

"I need some air," Paige said and bolted for the back door.

She crossed the cluttered veranda and climbed down the stairs. The night air felt crisp and clear. She welcomed the way it stung her bare arms and legs. It felt cleansing after the claustrophobic stuffiness of the kitchen. She moved away from the stairs and took a couple of steps off the path, putting distance between herself and the house.

The smell of damp grass and chicken poo filled her nose. She could see the outline of a Hills Hoist a few metres away and the dark shadows of outbuildings. The baby moved in her belly as if joyful to be out in the open and free of the house. Paige put her hand on her swollen abdomen. She'd been so worked up, she hadn't stopped to think how all this might be affecting her child. Hal needed her, but so did the baby. She had to calm down. Maybe it was time to just let go and trust that tomorrow would be soon enough to get help.

Paige looked up at the black expanse above. The stars glinted sharp and clear as if only metres away. She took a deep breath and turned back to the house. Lizzy enjoyed being right more than being liked. Paige had a feeling that Soona wasn't the only one with a few bats in her belfry. Even so, the woman was doing her best to help Hal.

She decided that the best way to deal with Lizzy might be to humour her. Paige began nodding her head unaware of the movement. *By this time tomorrow, we'll be miles away.* She squared her shoulders and headed back up the stairs.

Chapter Five

Hal became aware of something brushing his wrist. He tried to move his arm and touch Paige's shoulder, but found his wrist clamped and held down. He opened his eyes to a bright light; fuzzy and shifting. The effort of lifting his head set off a dull throb.

"Paige?" he asked, his tongue sticking to the roof of his mouth.

"No. But you're in good hands," a voice answered, but the timbre of the voice was harsh and far from reassuring.

Hal tried to sit up and realised he was restrained by something thick and tight around his chest. "What's going on? Where's my wife?" he asked, pulling at the restraint.

He tried to push himself up and an explosion of agony erupted in his leg. The pain, red hot, reached all the way from his foot to his groin. He sagged back onto the bed and ground his teeth.

"Out of one to ten, how would you rate your pain?" The voice asked.

His mouth formed words, but he couldn't catch his breath. Between gasps, he tried to remember where he was, but the grinding agony of his leg blotted out all but the present.

He felt a hand on his forehead. "Paige?" Even as he called her name, his senses told him the hand was too large and coarse to be his wife's.

He felt something cold touch his arm and then a sharp sting. He wanted to move his head, but fear of disturbing his leg kept him frozen in place.

"I've given you something for the pain. You'll be able to sleep now."

Heavy footfalls moved away from the bed. "Wait," Hal called. "Where's my wife?"

The fuzzy light grew and Hal realised a door had opened. What at first looked blurry, coalesced into an outline surrounded by light. The back light made it difficult to gauge whether a man or woman stood in the doorway, but Hal was sure the voice belonged to a female.

"She's fine. Just getting her beauty sleep. You'd better do the same." The doorknob rattled. "I'll be back in the wee hours."

The door closed and apart from a thin line at the bottom of the door, the room fell into darkness. He watched the bar of light and waited for his eyes to adjust to the gloom. Things cleared. His last vivid memory was the snake. He remembered the shock of the bite and then the creature slithering out from under the car. After that, everything went white and curled up at the edges.

His eyes felt dry; lips droopy. His leg hurt, but in a faraway sense, as if it were attached to someone else – someone floating away. Whatever the woman had given him was certainly fast acting. He let his eyes close. A snapshot of a grey-haired woman waving her arm and saying "Mable House" filled his mind. He focused on the woman, her face elongated and her eyes bulged until she looked like a ghoul. Her lower jaw gaped open and a dark green snake slithered out.

Hal's eyes snapped open. He found the thin yellow bar under the door and let out a breath. He watched the light, grateful for the comfort it offered. His lids closed again.

He summoned a picture of Paige in his mind. She lay back in a pool lounger, her head turned towards him and her blue eyes framed by golden lashes, sprinkled with sea salt. Around her, Hal could see white sand. She gave a half smile and the smattering of freckles over her nose danced. He held on to the image for as long as he could before sleep took him.

* * *

Paige lay on a narrow metal-framed bed. She didn't know what time it was. Late probably. Or very early. She pulled the sheet and heavy woollen blanket up to her chin and closed her eyes. She couldn't coax her mind to rest. Usually sleep came like a warm tunnel, all she had to do was close her eyes and let the soft darkness take her. Those blissful nights seemed far away, like a half-forgotten dream. Every time she closed her eyes, Hal's screams chased her back to wakefulness.

The baby was restless, shifting and kicking as though sharing her distress. Paige turned on her side and draped her arm over her belly. Getting pregnant had been neither planned nor unplanned. Something that just happened. One minute both her and Hal were newlyweds and the next, they were soon to be parents. From the moment they found out, Hal had been thrilled.

Paige smiled in the darkness. He'd make an amazing father. Once they got back home, their new life would begin. Leaving Melbourne to be near Hal's elderly father in Perth had been easier than she thought. It had been hard to leave her friends at work and her Aunty Enid, but the plane trip only took three and a half hours. Once Hal's leg healed and the baby was old enough, they could visit.

The room lay in almost total darkness, she could just make out the window and the grey chink of moonlight slipping past the curtains. Paige wished she could sleep in the same room as Hal, they hadn't slept apart since they were married, and she missed the comforting rhythm of his breathing. It seemed odd that Lizzy had put him on the third floor when the paramedics would have to move him again tomorrow.

Everything about this place is odd, Paige thought groggily. Her mind wanted to relive the day's horrific events, but her eyelids drooped and sleep overtook her.

* * *

The sound of birds piping brought Hal close to waking. Their relentless chatter pierced a soft point in his subconscious and he began to surface. His mind resisted the call back to reality until the pain in his lower leg pushed through his defences. Hal groaned and opened his eyes.

One window in the tiny room, narrow and draped with some sort of ruffled yellow curtain, provided the only natural light. Weak rays of sunlight filtered in and cast a long rectangle on the dusty wooden boards. Judging by the fragile glow, Hal guessed it must be early morning.

He turned his head, slowly as if its movement was directly attached to his leg.

"You're awake," Paige said.

She sat on a folding metal chair pulled near the left side of his bed, her blonde hair sleep-tousled. One delicate hand rested over her belly. He could see the worry and fear etched into the dark smudges under her eyes. He'd caused that worry.

"Sorry," he said, speaking his thoughts aloud.

Paige's brow creased. "You've nothing to be sorry for." She leaned forward and put her hand over his. "How do you feel?"

"Not too bad." He swallowed. "Could use a drink of water."

A short metal locker stood next to the bed, on top a jug of water and a single glass. Paige stood and poured. He pulled himself up onto his elbows. Last night he'd felt thick straps pinning him in place, he wondered if it had been a dream or something to keep him from thrashing around and further injuring his leg. He noticed Paige's

42

sidelong look and tried not to wince. She held the glass to his mouth and tipped it for him to drink.

"Where are we?" he asked when he lay back on the pillow. "What is this place?"

"The woman that stopped to help us, Lizzy, this is her house." Paige returned the glass to the cabinet and sat down. "She drove us back here to use her phone, but when I tried it," she paused and closed her eyes for a second. "It didn't work."

Hal looked down, taking in the drip running from his arm to the stand beside the bed. "I don't get it. I thought I was in some kind of hospital." He motioned to the drip and the cage tenting the blankets over his legs.

"This place used to be a hospital," Paige nodded. "And Lizzy is a nurse. She's been treating you since we arrived here last night." She stopped talking and ran her hand through her hair. "I know it's all a bit strange, but I didn't have any choice. There were no other cars around. My phone wouldn't work." She held her hands up, palms out. "I didn't know what else to do."

Hal reached out and grabbed Paige's hand. "You did the right thing." He held her gaze and waited. She gave a slight nod. "You had no other choice. It beats spending the night in the bush, right? Or me dying?"

"Yeah." She gave a little laugh. The sound came close to a sob. "Lizzy's going to drive me to the nearest roadhouse this morning so I can call an ambulance. I'll be gone for a few hours, but hopefully, by tonight you'll be in a proper hospital."

"Listen, Paige," Hal said, raising himself onto one elbow. "Be careful when you're with that woman, we don't know anything about her." The effort of talking and trying to sit up made his vision blur and his leg blaze with fresh agony.

"I'll be fine, Hal." Paige stood and eased his shoulder back onto the bed. "You look flushed. Don't keep trying to get up."

"Just promise me you'll be careful." He didn't want to frighten his wife or put her through any more stress, but he'd seen active duty in a war zone and he'd learned to feel danger in the air. Sensing when to take extra care could often be the difference between life and death. He didn't know enough about their current situation to gauge just how much danger they were in, but his gut told him things weren't adding up.

Paige leaned over and kissed him. A soft gentle kiss that made him want to wrap his arms around her and stop her from leaving. Instead, he pulled her back and kissed her a second time.

"I need to check your drip and take a look at that leg," Lizzy said from the doorway.

Paige pulled away from him as though she'd been caught doing something wrong. Hal frowned. He didn't like the way she reacted to Lizzy's presence. Paige was kind and gentle, but not easily intimidated.

"Okay, just give us a minute," Hal said and was surprised to see Paige's eyes widen with shock.

"No, Hal. Let Lizzy do it now," she said and gave him a warning look.

Lizzy's washed out eyes fell on Hal. "I can't wait around all day," she said with a hint of impatience. "Do you want me to check your leg or not?"

"Yes. Thanks," he said and caught a grateful look from Paige.

Lizzy approached the bed and flung back the sheet. The cool air touched his skin and Hal felt a spark of pain in his ankle. He heard Paige gasp, and looked down. It was the first time he'd seen his legs since the snake bite, and what he saw took his breath away.

His right leg looked normal apart from the white bandage mid-way between his ankle and knee. His left leg was so swollen that the skin looked ready to burst. A blood-soaked bandage covered the skin just above his ankle. Beneath it, rose a knot of swelling the size of a fist.

His foot, the colour of an over-ripe plum, and the whole lower leg, lay encased in crude splints held in place with bandages.

"Hmm," Lizzy said and leaned closer to his broken leg. To Hal's horror, she sniffed. "No sign of infection yet," she said and pulled the sheet back up. "I'll give you something for the pain and bring you the bed pan," she said as she settled the sheets around Hal's chest.

He wanted to tell her to forget the painkillers. He didn't want to disappear back into the greyness of the previous night. He needed to be alert, but the strain of talking and trying to sit up zapped him of any strength, and the pain in his leg rapidly grew from red-hot to white. In truth, a part of him wanted to float away.

He nodded. "Thanks," he managed.

Lizzy disappeared into the small cupboard on the left of Hal's bed. He glanced over at Paige, struck by how pale she looked. He realised the sight of his leg had affected her as much as it had him. He clenched his lips together and swallowed. His wife's distress, coupled with pain and fatigue, threatened to overwhelm him. He laid his forearm over his eyes so Paige wouldn't see the building tears.

Lizzy reappeared and slid a small needle into the muscle of his upper arm. Soon he drifted off, voices seemed distant, movement and touch dream-like in its slowness. He was vaguely aware of Paige whispering something in his ear. It sounded like "moo pong", but could have been "hold on." He chuckled and closed his eyes.

Chapter Six

The ute still sat parked around the side of the house. Paige followed Lizzy along the same stone path she'd walked the night before, only now sunshine blanketed the property rather than darkness. Paige stepped over a cracked stone. In between glancing at the path and her surroundings, she took in details hidden in the night. Weeds and dandelions sprouted from the overgrown lawn. The house revealed itself to be in worse shape than she thought. The once red brick structure had faded to the colour of stale gingerbread. The veranda sagged drunkenly to the right and some of the many windows were boarded over. The overall effect came close to derelict.

Paige watched Lizzy's back as the woman marched towards the old Holden. Dressed in navy blue pants and a lighter blue loose shirt with short sleeves, it was as though Lizzy had donned her nursing clothes to properly inhabit her role. The fabric of the shirt strained against the woman's broad shoulders. Paige found herself hurrying in order to keep up with her long strides.

Once in the car, Lizzy turned to her and spoke for the first time since leaving the house. "When's the baby due?"

Caught off guard by the question, Paige hesitated. It was the first time Lizzy had made mention of Paige's obvious pregnancy, which in itself seemed strange. A big baby bump was usually the first thing people talked about. But until that moment, Lizzy had managed to avoid the subject.

"Two months." Paige put her hand on the swelling.

"Not long," Lizzy said, looking not at Paige, but straight ahead at the windscreen.

"No. Not long," Paige agreed and wondered if it would be rude to ask her to hurry up and drive.

Lizzy tapped a thick finger to her lip as if thinking. A few seconds ticked by and then she put the key in the ignition. The engine clicked a few times, but refused to start. Paige gripped the hem of her dress and waited while Lizzy tried again. A metallic grinding filled the cab, then nothing.

Paige shook her head. "What's wrong? Why won't it start?" Her voice rose, the frustration jagged in her words.

Lizzy shrugged. "Probably the starter motor."

"What's that? Can you fix it?" Paige asked, turning her body towards Lizzy.

Lizzy reached under the seat and pulled out a large silver spanner. For a terrifying second, Paige thought she meant to hit her with it. Then Lizzy pulled the release lever next to the steering wheel.

"Wait here," she said and got out of the cab.

Paige bit her lip and watched Lizzy lift the bonnet. Paige whispered a litany of curses under her breath. She jumped when she heard a metal crack.

"Slide over and try turning it on." Lizzy's voice came from under the bonnet.

Paige slid sideways, lifting one leg at a time over the gear stick. Squeezing herself behind the wheel, she called out, "Now?"

"Yes. Turn the keys and press on the accelerator."

Paige held her breath and did as instructed, trying to ignore the growing certainty that the ute wouldn't start. Again the grind of metal and clicking rose from under the bonnet, but the engine didn't catch. Paige lowered her head onto the steering wheel and closed her eyes.

"I'll tell Soona to take a look at it." Lizzy's voice next to the window startled her.

Paige lifted her head and regarded the woman. She looked unfazed by the car's failure to start. *She knew it wouldn't start, she's not at all surprised.* Paige didn't know where that thought came from, but she had no doubt it was true. For whatever reason, Lizzy wanted her two new guests to stay put.

"Do you have another car?" Paige asked without any real hope.

Lizzy pulled the driver's door open. "Does it look like I have a fleet of cars?" she asked, and wheeled her arm around.

"No, I didn't mean…" Paige tried to explain.

"I know it's difficult for you and Mr November, the calendar boy up there to understand," Lizzy pointed at the house. "But I'm not made of money. I've done everything possible for you and all you do is look down your nose at me." Spittle flew out of her mouth, narrowly missing Paige's face.

Lizzy turned and stomped back to the house leaving Paige sitting behind the wheel of the useless vehicle with her mouth open. She tried to work her mind around what just happened but kept returning to whether Lizzy had done something to the ute to make sure it wouldn't start or not. It seemed like insanity. Then she recalled the angry outburst. Paige replayed Lizzy's words over in her mind. *She called Hal, Mr November. Where does that level of anger and resentment come from?*

That led her to another frightening thought. *Did Lizzy know the phone wouldn't work?* Had she brought Paige and Hal here knowing they wouldn't be able to call for help?

Maybe. Almost certainly. Paige rubbed her hand over her mouth. What she couldn't get her mind around was why? Why would the woman want to keep them against their will? *Maybe she's going to kill us,* a little voice in her head whispered. Paige pushed away that thought. If she wanted to kill them, she wouldn't be trying to nurse Hal back to health. *But is she?* Yes. Paige thought so, but she wasn't a doctor. She had no idea if what Lizzy was doing was really helping Hal.

Her pulse rate increased. Her heart wasn't pounding, but it beat faster. She needed to get Hal the hell out of this cuckoo hatch and into a hospital. She rubbed her hands together and then steepled them under her chin. The question was, what lengths would Lizzy go to in order to keep them here? Paige didn't want to believe the woman might be dangerous, but could she be sure?

She drummed her fingers on the wheel and looked around the cab. It occurred to her that the Holden might not drive, but their Ford would. *If I can change the tyre.* Paige slid gracelessly out of the ute and slammed the door. After Lizzy's angry outburst, Paige wondered what to expect. One thing she *was* sure of, Lizzy wouldn't be happy when Paige told her she intended to leave. She stopped walking. From her current vantage point she could see the back door; over to the left of the house, a ramshackle chook pen with at least four birds pottering around; beyond the outbuildings stood patches of trees and long grass. Paige decided it would be too easy to get lost in a place like this and tried to let the idea go.

* * *

When she entered the kitchen, Lizzy stood at the sink. She tipped a yellow and black kettle under the running water. She didn't look up or acknowledge Paige in any way. The tightness of the woman's shoulders and thrust of her long chin told Paige the storm was far from over.

"I'm sorry if I sound ungrateful. I know how much you've helped me and especially Hal." Paige watched Lizzy

49

put the kettle on the stove top and light a match to the burner. The heavy aroma of gas filled the room.

"I just got … well, a bit panicky." Paige continued. "I … Thank you for helping us. I really mean it." She bit her lower lip and prayed she sounded grateful, with maybe just a touch of fear. The last shouldn't be difficult as she could feel its dark tendrils creeping up on her.

"Alright then," Lizzy said without turning around.

Paige wasn't sure if she'd won the woman over. In fact, she didn't think Lizzy liked her either, and the scornful way she'd referred to Hal made her even more puzzled about the woman's intentions.

The screen door slapped open and Soona ambled into the kitchen carrying a cereal box that had been cut in half. She wore the same denim dungarees as the day before, but underneath sported a brown sweatshirt strained across her thick upper body. Paige could see the box contained four brown speckled eggs. Soona put them down on the table with surprising gentleness and then headed for the drawing room.

"Stop!" Lizzy turned from the stove and fixed her glare on Soona.

Soona stopped moving and hunched her shoulders together as if expecting a blow. It was a small movement for the large woman. If Paige had disliked Lizzy before, that flinch of fear in Soona's shoulders turned her dislike to contempt. Suddenly the room felt too small, and the two women like giants. Paige was caught in the middle of whatever drama these two women played. She didn't want to look at Lizzy or Soona, but she couldn't tear her eyes away.

"What's in your pocket?" Lizzy asked.

Soona shook her head, her dark hair clung to her forehead and cheeks in damp strings. Lizzy's lips bunched together in an angry pucker. Her eyes, the colour of shark's skin, narrowed. The hairs on Paige's arms tingled. She could almost see the storm gathering behind Lizzy's eyes.

Paige felt the urge to say or do something to break the tension, but her mouth felt dry and a small part of her feared Lizzy would unleash the storm on her.

Lizzy crossed the room, her sensible brown lace-ups thumping the boards hard enough to shake the table. Soona opened her mouth and let out a sound that reminded Paige of a baby horse. Lizzy grabbed a handful of Soona's shirt, probably a chunk of skin with it, and spun her around.

Lizzy plunged her hand into the front pocket of Soona's dungarees and pulled out an egg. She held it in the palm of her hand.

"What have I told you?" Lizzy asked, pushing the egg under Soona's nose.

Soona's hands flapped at her sides as if she were trying to take flight. Lizzy's hand flipped up and smashed the egg into Soona's forehead, grinding and rubbing it against the woman's skin. The centre of Soona's face was coated in yellow sticky goo that dribbled off her chin and pooled on her sweatshirt.

Lizzy stepped back and inspected the mess. "Get in your room and clean yourself up." Lizzy gave the woman's shoulder a shove with enough force to send her stumbling into the drawing room.

Lizzy turned back to Paige and gave her head a small shake. The change from barely contained rage to parental disapproval took seconds. In that moment, Paige knew she was in trouble. The air felt hot, like a heavy blanket had been thrown over her. A tingling sensation jangled her nerves. Paige pressed her lips together to keep them from trembling, and tried to keep her face smooth and impassive.

"She's always sneaking eggs." A sad, almost motherly smile pulled up the sides of her mouth. "She thinks if she keeps them warm a chick will hatch. I've tried to tell her that we don't have a rooster, but she's retarded so I suppose she has trouble understanding."

51

Paige tried to think of something to say. "Oh." The sound slipped out of her mouth and even to her own ears it sounded like a weak puff. She'd just watched Lizzy bully and assault a woman whose intelligence was like that of a small child. She felt disgust at herself for watching and staying mute, *and* at Lizzy for the obvious pleasure she took in hurting someone mentally incapable of protecting themselves.

"You don't have that problem, do you?" Lizzy pointed at Paige's belly and made a sound that came close to being a laugh.

"What?" Paige asked, confused by the woman's sudden change of tone and direction.

"You've got a rooster," she said and made a wet snorting sound with her nose.

Paige could feel the heat creeping up her neck. She put her hand on her belly instinctively covering it from Lizzy's pointing finger. She tried to think of a response that wouldn't make the woman angry, but Lizzy had already lost interest in the conversation and returned to making a cup of tea.

"I think I'll go and sit with Hal for a while," Paige said, trying to sound casual.

"Don't wander around too much up there, some of those rooms aren't safe," she said without turning around.

Chapter Seven

Hal could hear a voice coming from above like droplets of rain under the shelter of a tree. Beneath him, the airbed rocked gently on the waves; he could see the white shoreline and smell the salt in the air. He wanted to paddle back, but his leg felt like it was caught in the jaws of something solid and unyielding. *If I'm floating on the ocean, how can raindrops be falling out of a tree?* His mind struggled to make sense of the voice and the jaws. Both were very real.

"Hal."

He heard his name and the shoreline wavered. If he turned his head, he knew the sun and the waves would disappear. He wasn't sure how he knew this, it was just a certainty. Like the way he knew that if he turned on a tap, water would come out.

"Hal, please."

He recognised the cadence and reluctantly let go of the shimmering vista and turned to the sound of his wife's voice. His eyes opened and, for a second, no longer than the time it took to blink, he thought he was on the beach in Bali and his wife was leaning in to kiss him. He could taste the salt on her lips and hear the distant cry of seagulls.

"Hal, I need you to wake up." The urgency in her voice swept the gulls away and brought him back to the tiny room.

"Paige," his voice slurred. "Are you okay?" This time the words were clearer.

His mind still felt heavy, but now he could make out details. He was still in the small hospital room. Paige, heavily pregnant, stood next to the bed. She wore the white sundress she'd had on, when? He tried to remember when he'd last seen her. Hours ago or had days passed?

"Hal, I'm going to get you out of here." He watched her mouth move and tried to keep up with her words.

"I think we might be in deep shit," she said and leaned closer to his ear.

He could feel her hair tickle his nose. He wanted to laugh, but his woolly mind slowly made sense of what she was saying. *Deep shit.*

He wanted to ask her what sort of shit when she spoke again. "I'm going to sneak out and walk back to our car." Her voice a whisper, so close to his ear he could feel her breath on his neck.

"I'll have to change the tyre myself so you need to talk me through it."

"You can't do that," he said, sounding more like himself. "You've never changed a tyre and ..." he paused. Even pumped full of dope, he realised that what he said next would make him sound like an asshole.

"And what?" Paige asked.

"And you're pregnant," he said, and winced at the look of hurt he'd put on his wife's face.

"Listen to me very carefully, Hal," her voice dropped low, a notch deeper than he was used to hearing. "The woman who brought us here is crazy. Not just a little bit, but big time crazy." Paige drew in a long breath; he could feel it rush past his cheek. "She's keeping us here. I don't know why, but right now I don't care." She put her hand on his cheek and looked him in the eyes. "All I care about is getting you out of here, so you'd better start explaining the finer points of changing a tyre."

He could see the fear swimming in her eyes and he felt a hollow sensation in the pit of his stomach. The haze cleared and the gravity of their predicament dawned on him. *You knew you were in trouble the moment you saw that woman.* Yes, but the pain had been in charge, and when the pain leads the way the only thing that matters is making it stop.

His head felt clear now, but the sizzling fingers swarming up from his ankle still gave him a run for his money. He made himself focus on Paige's eyes.

"I already took off the damaged wheel so you only need to put on the spare."

When he'd finished explaining, he made Paige repeat the process back to him.

"Okay," she said. "I'm going to try to slip out without either of them seeing me."

Hal held up his hand. "Wait, what do you mean either of them? Who else is here?"

Paige grimaced. "There's another woman, Soona. I think she's autistic." She shook her head. "I don't know what their relationship is, but it's creepy. I don't like leaving you with them, but I've racked my brains and this is the best I can come up with."

Hal noticed faint purple smudges under his wife's eyes and a tremor in her voice. He should be the one taking care of her, she was due to give birth in two months and here he lay sending her out to rescue them.

"Maybe we should wait," he said. "Give it a few more days. By then my leg might be a bit better and I could come with you." He didn't believe it even as the words came out of his mouth. He suspected his tubular and fibular were broken, he'd seen similar injuries stationed in Afghanistan, and he knew it would take surgery and months of physio to come back from something like this.

"No. It has to be now," Paige said. "You need proper medical help." She paused and looked over her shoulder as if she expected Lizzy to burst through the door. "She wants us here for a reason and I don't want to hang around to find out what it is."

He knew she was right, but it didn't make it any easier. "Don't take any unnecessary risks. If you can't walk all the way to the car or the tyre's too heavy for you to lift, come back and we'll think of something else." He wanted to add watch out for snakes, but after yesterday, she didn't need reminding.

"Okay." She nodded. "I'm going now. If Lizzy asks, tell her I'm sleeping. Last night she stuck me downstairs in a freaky hospital dormitory. Hopefully she'll assume I'm in there." She paused and seemed to be thinking. "Try to keep her talking, but be careful, she gets angry over anything."

She bent and pressed her lips against his. Her mouth felt soft and warm. He hooked his arm around her back and pulled her down until her breasts were pressed against his chest.

"Be careful. I love you," he said in a croaky whisper.

"I love you too," she said, and pulled back.

Without a backward glance, she was gone.

* * *

Hal watched the back of the door; he wasn't sure how long he stared at the flaking paint and the round tarnished knob – maybe an hour? When he looked back over at the small, dirt-stained window, the sun had crept halfway across the room. His leg jangled with pain. Whatever Lizzy had given him wore off fast.

His gaze shifted over to the narrow cupboard doorway. He recalled Lizzy pushing a trolley out from there and wondered if she kept the drugs there too. He felt a stab of shame. With his pregnant wife trekking through the bush to get him help, all he could think about was getting his next shot of happy juice.

He laid his forearm over his eyes and tried to think of something other than the agony below his knee. He needed to pee. He looked over at the metal locker next to his bed. A tall glass half-filled with water would have to do as a makeshift bedpan. He pulled himself up onto his elbows and shrieked. The tiniest pull on his leg made his bones grind together.

Hal gritted his teeth and stretched out his hand. His fingers were closing around the glass when the door banged open and Lizzy strode into the room. Hal felt ridiculously pleased to see her. So much so he suddenly felt like crying.

"How's the pain?" she asked by way of greeting.

She held a tray, which she put down on the locker. He could see a plate with what looked like scrambled eggs and a syringe.

"It's bad," he said, eyes locked on the syringe. His stomach growled, but he barely noticed.

Lizzy looked him over with flat emotionless eyes. "I'd better take a look at you."

Hal forced himself not to flinch or cry out as she flipped back the sheet. He didn't look down at his leg, not wanting another close-up of the carnage he'd seen on last inspection. After what seemed like an eternity, she pulled the sheet back up.

"I'm going to have to clean your wound and stitch it closed." Hal listened to her speak, but as hard as he tried to concentrate on what she was saying, his eyes kept drifting back to the syringe. The liquid inside it looked clear and the tip of the needle practically gleamed in the light.

"It'll be painful, so I'll give you something before I start." She thought for a moment. "Do you need to use the bottle?"

"Yes, but I can wait until you've given me the injection," he said hoping she couldn't hear the

desperation in his voice. *Just give me the fucking painkillers.*
"The pain's bad."

She balled her hands into fists and wedged them above her sizable hips. "No. First things first. If you wet the bed, I'll have to lift you and change the sheets." She leaned her head forward slightly, craning her neck and jutting out her chin. "You might not care, but I do."

She moved around the bed and opened the cupboard door. Her head disappeared inside for a moment and then she reappeared holding a plastic bottle with a long, wide neck and a flat bottom.

"Let's get this nasty business out of the way and then we can make you more comfortable."

After Hal finished peeing into the bottle, Lizzy took it and scurried out of the room. He heard the sound of running water hitting something metal and then a clanging. He couldn't remember how he'd gotten into the room and didn't know what sort of building he was in, other than its obvious age. Having no frame of reference made him feel oddly disoriented, as if he were in a bubble that could be drifting in space. The only indication that he was still in the real world came from the sunshine that spilled through the window.

He strained to hear other noises and became aware of a distant rattling. Somewhere in the big blue sky beyond his view, a bird twittered.

"Right," Lizzy said entering the room. Her voice had a sonorous quality that made it sound almost masculine. "I'm going to put this in with your drip." She picked up the syringe and waved it near his face.

When she'd finished administering the painkiller, Hal let out a long breath and closed his eyes. He could feel the edges of the world beginning to blur and his mind slipping into a soothing darkness.

"No you don't," Lizzy said and slapped him on the cheek.

His eyes popped opened. "What are you doing?" Even through the haze he managed to feel surprised that the woman had actually hit him.

Deep shit. That's what Paige had said they were in. But how deep, he couldn't say. He wondered if Paige had made it to the car yet. It must have been at least an hour since she left.

"You're going to eat some eggs before you sleep," Lizzy took the plate from the tray. "You're so dopey, I'll have to feed you," she said and plopped down in the chair that Paige had occupied earlier.

"Okay," he said, then added, "Thank you, Lizzy."

She paused with the spoon halfway to his mouth. Her forehead creased with annoyance. Her eyebrows were black, peppered with grey. The colour matched her weird eyes, he thought crazily. "Your wife should be the one spoon-feeding you. I've got plenty to do without babying you."

He could see her mind working. Any second, she'd put the spoon down and go looking for Paige. He had to keep her busy as long as possible. "She was beat, so she went to lie down," he said, and tried for a smile.

Lizzy's eyes moved over his face and then down to his wrist. She studied the tattoo for a moment. "Why do people feel the need to mark themselves like that?" she asked, and gestured with the spoon.

It seemed like, for the moment, she'd forgotten about Paige. Her shifting thoughts unnerved him, but at least her attention had been diverted. Hal wondered how long it would be before Paige returned with help. Lizzy gave him the heebie-jeebies, but he couldn't tell if she was dangerous.

"I don't know why I got the tattoo," he said, answering her question. "It's just one of those things that seem like a good idea at the time."

"Like travelling around in the bush with your pregnant wife?" She fixed him with a look of grim disapproval.

The aggressiveness of her words took him by surprise. He could feel the painkillers starting to sweep him away, making it difficult to focus on what she said.

"Maybe," he said and felt the room soften. The hard edges of the door frame and the sunlight on the floor looked fuzzy.

Lizzy shovelled a spoon of eggs into his mouth and he swallowed automatically. The taste it left on his tongue was thick and unpleasant. He wondered what she'd put in them. Before he had time to consider what she'd done to ruin the eggs, she shoved another spoonful into mouth. He resisted the urge to gag, and swallowed.

"Alright. That will do for now," she said and set the plate aside. She gave him the glass and allowed him two sips before it disappeared from his hand.

"I'll get rid of the dishes and then start on your leg." It sounded ominous. Hal wondered what *start on your leg* would mean in terms of pain. She'd mentioned cleaning and stitching his wound; he was grateful the drugs were taking effect and could only hope she intended to give him a local before she got to the stitching part. Insanely, thinking about Lizzy stitching made him want to laugh.

He closed his eyes and allowed himself to drift. He pictured Paige, alone, walking through the bush. In his mind he could clearly see the sunlight glinting off her golden hair. He permitted himself a moment to consider her perfection before the guilt of letting her go off into the unknown overtook him.

Lizzy was crazy, but she was right, it had been his idea to drive to the South West without any real plan. He'd wanted a few more weeks, just the two of them, before the baby arrived. It was selfish of him, and now Paige had to pay the price. *We could've just spent a week at a lodge, why did I insist on discovering the Wild West?* The simple answer, he wanted to be free one last time before the baby took over their lives.

A haze crawled over his conscious mind, trying to pull him down into the dark. He tried to force himself to remain alert, didn't deserve the comfort of oblivion, not while his wife and unborn baby struggled to find help. Thirty seconds later, sleep took him.

* * *

"Where is she?" The words hit him like a slap. He remembered Lizzy slapping him earlier and opened his eyes.

The sunlight waned. Long shadows cast by the window spread a gloom. He shifted his head left and saw Lizzy standing over him. Looking up at her, the loose creases of skin under her chin framed angry spots of red filling her cheeks.

"She's gone," Lizzy said. "And I bet you put her up to it."

He tried to think of something to say, but his thoughts were scattered and his mouth felt packed with cotton wool. Lizzy moved to the end of the bed and pulled back the sheets. He winced as the cool air hit his leg.

"Grab his shoulders."

He tried to sit up and ask whose shoulders she meant, but something slid under his neck. It took him a moment to realise someone else stood in the room. A face swam above him. He took in a slack mouth and dark empty eyes. The thick smell of eggs and unwashed hair filled his nostrils. He grimaced and tried to pull away, but the woman with her arm under his neck held tight.

He knew he had the strength to shake her off, but as he struggled, hands wrapped around his ankles. His legs lifted and all thoughts of resistance vanished. A sheet of agony enveloped him; he screamed.

"No. No don't," he heard himself begging, and almost didn't recognise his own voice.

Hal felt himself being lifted off the bed. The bones in his lower leg ground together and the world darkened. He seemed to hang in mid-air for a moment and then his butt hit something, the rest of his body quickly followed. He tried to rock forward and grab his leg, but his shoulders were pressed down. Something slid across his body and he felt pinned in place.

He looked above him and could see faces. Lizzy's and the other woman's floating eerily. He began to understand that he was on a stretcher and a fleeting memory of being in this position before came to him.

"What are you doing?" He managed to get the words out through clenched teeth.

Lizzy glanced down and regarded him with emotionless, shark eyes. "That snake bite's infected. We need to take your leg off or it'll kill you."

The words sliced through the pain. *Did she say "take your leg off?"* Yellow ceiling sped by; the trolley was moving.

"You're not cutting my leg off," he shrieked and pushed against the restraints that held him on the stretcher.

A door banged and he was in another room. The powerful smell of bleach stung his nose. A large metal sink loomed on his right. He turned his head and saw a silver trolley laid out with evil looking instruments – in the centre, a hacksaw. It had a solid handle, the blade slightly rusty.

"No." It came out as more of a scream than a word.

Lizzy's face appeared above him. She leaned so close that for one crazy moment, he thought she meant to kiss him. He could smell her sour breath.

"Settle down. I'm only taking the lower leg.

Chapter Eight

Paige pulled on the sides of her denim jacket and grabbed the phone out of her bra so she could check the time: nearly midday. Forty minutes since leaving Mable House. Snatches of pale blue sky were visible above the canopy. A crispness hung in the air that the weak glimpses of sunlight did nothing to warm.

When she'd snuck out the back door, Lizzy was upstairs and Soona nowhere in sight. Paige worked her way around the house until she made it back to the ute, then grabbed her jacket out of the back and headed to the left side of the house, avoiding the entry road at the front of the building. Her plan had been to duck into the bush and try to walk parallel to the road.

The uneven terrain and scattered debris from the trees made walking a challenge. She looked back over her shoulder. Behind her, as ahead, only scraggy looking shrubs, twisted trees, and deep native grass flourished. All around her patches of pink, purple, and yellow wildflowers poked their heads up in recognition of the spring sunshine. Paige supposed the setting might be considered pretty, and under different circumstances she'd likely stop and enjoy the wildness of it all. But for the moment, all she could think about was water.

She didn't bring any with her, telling herself not to waste time trying to find something to carry it in. *What a mistake that had been.* Her throat felt dry and her lips cracked. She tried to remind herself that a human being could go for three days without water, but her parched tongue told her otherwise. She thought of the Esky sitting in the back of the Ford: cans of cola and bottles of water inside. All would be warm by now, but even warm they'd taste wonderful to her sandy mouth.

She heard a crackle and scanned the long grass ahead for signs of movement, but found it impossible to tell if anything slithered beneath the thick foliage. Paige looked to her left and could make out the edge of the road between the trees. If she tried walking closer, she'd be torn to pieces on the thorny branches of the yellow bushes blooming there. Those bushes reminded her of everything else about his place. They looked appealing and harmless, but close up they were surprisingly sharp.

She sidestepped the area where she'd heard the rustling and continued forward. The drive from the cheese factory had taken about twenty minutes so, she guessed the walk back would take about an hour and ten. *Under normal circumstance.* Yes, if she were walking on the road and had some water, but struggling around thorny bushes and over fallen branches while grappling with thirst was a different story.

At the rate she progressed, she wouldn't reach the car for at least another hour. She wondered how Hal was holding up. He'd done his best to seem calm, but Paige heard the pain in his voice. He'd tried to talk her out of fixing the car, but they both knew it was the only way. She prayed he'd be okay, and that God would help her be strong enough to reach the car and do what she had to. She didn't know what Lizzy might be capable of or if the woman really *was* dangerous, but her gut told her she had to get Hal out of that house. The baby moved, a slow shifting unlike anything she'd felt before. Paige took it as a sign of agreement and picked up the pace.

She checked her phone again, looking for the time and the dim possibility of a signal. She puffed out a deep breath, ten after-twelve and no lit bars. She slipped the phone back in her bra and moved on. Her feet were swollen inside her shoes and her back strained as if under the weight of a ton of bricks, but the worst part had to be the itch growing around her calves. She guessed it was from insect bites and the constant friction of dry grass against her skin. *Why the hell did I wear a short sundress? Because*, she answered herself, *you thought you were going to be spending yesterday enjoying some alone time with your hubby, not slogging through the bush looking for help.*

When she made it to the car, the first thing she'd do, after drinking a few litres of water, was rub some Soothe on her legs. Another little promise she made to herself, another reward for taking one more painful step and then another.

To keep her mind occupied and stop herself thinking about water and snakes and all things fangs-ridden inhabiting the bush, she went over the steps Hal had taught her; *lift the tyre in place, put on the lug nuts in a star pattern. Next, tighten them lightly using her fingers, then put the remaining nuts on and tighten all using the torque wrench ...* It sounded simple. Hal made it sound easy. Paige swallowed and her throat rasped.

She needed to rest. Her heart thundered, labouring to pump the increased volume of blood around her body. Her breathing came in shallow puffs, and she neared the edge of exhaustion. Paige took another step; her foot caught on a piece of dead wood and she stumbled forward. Hands splayed out, she landed on them and her knees.

Hitting the ground with a jolt, her left hand landed centimetres from a jagged stick jutting from a fallen branch. Something shifted under her right hand, wet and slick. She pulled back and made a sound of disgust. Her hand came away coated in blackish red goo. Where she'd landed lay the rotting remains of what might have been a galah. The bird's stomach had burst and clusters of maggots writhed around the spill of intestines.

Paige shrieked, scuttling backward on her hands and knees. She could feel the sludge on her palm, sticky and wet. Leaning back on her knees, she rubbed her hand on the fallen leaves. Finally daring to look, her palm was stained brown and smelt thick with decay. Her stomach lurched and she spent the next few minutes heaving up a mixture of water and chunks of bread.

When she managed to stop gagging, she spat and wiped her arm across her mouth. The smell of her hand set off another wave of nausea. Her stomach clenched and her eyes watered, but mercifully the vomiting subsided. Paige sat back, ignoring the crunching leaves under her weight, and tried not to think about whatever insects might be crawling just out of sight.

She closed her eyes and took three, deep, shuddering breaths. She had to keep it together, stay calm, even though her skin crawled and she had the urge to run screaming back to the house. *It's just a dead bird for Christ's sake.* Trying to stand, the movement set off waves of dizziness that made her head spin. She knew she couldn't afford to risk another fall, if she hadn't caught herself and landed on her hands and knees, her stomach would've hit the ground. What then? *I'd have hurt my baby.*

She drew her knees up as far as her belly would allow and lowered her head. Paige knew she should be moving, keeping her momentum going, but her body felt tired and sluggish. If she pushed any harder the baby would be the one to suffer. Trying to sort out the possibilities in her mind, she gave her head a shake. If she didn't hurry, Lizzy would notice her absence and ... Her thinking faltered. What would Lizzy do? *Take it out on Hal.* Hadn't she known all along that's what might happen?

It seemed crazy, but she pictured Lizzy smashing that egg on Soona's forehead. The action so sudden and cruel, *it was scary. Scary. That's the word that best described Lizzy. You saw it the minute she stopped the car,* a small voice in her head whispered. Yes, Paige had seen it, but that little spark of recognition, the feeling in the pit of your stomach that tells you you're in danger, was no match for panic and desperation. So she'd pushed the warning voice aside and grasped onto the offer of help. She thought of a line from an old movie, something about relying on the kindness of strangers. *Whoever thought of that never met Lizzy Hatcher.*

A bird squawked above. Paige lifted her head to a lone galah sitting in the low branches of a silver gum. It ruffled its grey and pink feathers and let out another cry. She wondered if it called to its dead mate. Her vision blurred with tears until the bird became no more than a fuzzy pink blob. The mournful sound of its cry touched her soul, and all the frustration and fear tumbled out in jagged sobs.

Eventually the tears subsided and Paige climbed to her feet. Hal depended on her to bring help, and she would do it if she had to walk all day. She checked left and could still see the edge of the road. Up ahead, the bush appeared dense and impenetrable, she'd have to go farther away from the road if she hoped to get through. Shrugging deeper into her jacket, Paige veered to the right.

Within minutes she came to a clearing, thick yellowish grass and wild flowers blanketed the ground, but the spikey shrubs and crouching trees were less tightly packed. The sun lit up the area like a spotlight, and for a moment, Paige paused and drank it in. Walking seemed blessedly easier now and the way was more direct. A tendril of worry crept into her mind, *what if I've strayed too far from the road?* The thought of being in the bush, in the dark, sent a flutter of panic through her. She decided to walk until she reached a cluster of grass trees that looked to be a few hundred metres ahead, and then she'd head back to the left.

When Paige approached the trees, she noticed something grey just beyond them. Not the washed-out grey of dead branches, but something metallic winking in the light. She pushed on past the grass trees and caught a whiff of peppermint. Her heart beat a little faster and she tried to pick up her pace. Wattle trees blocked her path so she pushed around to the right where she found a gap in the scrub. She had to lift her knees up and hop over some low hanging fronds. As she stumbled free, she found the metallic object that had caught her attention – the rim of a sagging cyclone wire-fence, and behind it what she knew must be the back of the cheese factory.

Paige grabbed the edge of the fence and squeezed, just to make sure it was real. She gave a little cry of triumph and then laughed at her own delight. *I made it, I got here. The nightmare's nearly over.* If she'd had the energy, she would've danced. Instead she clambered over the fence that now sagged to knee-level, and headed around the building.

Her pulse raced, she felt breathless, but energised. Paige wiped her forehead with her sleeve and followed the line of the building. The smell of peppermint was stronger now. She pictured the Ford standing under the trees with the doors open, their suitcases piled around the gaping hatch. For a split second she actually saw it. The burnt orange paintwork glittering under the sun's rays. The blue Esky with the white top sitting on the ground, beads of moisture rolling down the plastic sides.

But the image in her mind became a trick of her imagination, the ghost of what should've been. She rounded the corner of the building and stared, mouth open, at the empty carpark. The car and everything in it were gone. The cluster of peppermint trees with their branches rustling in the wind stood sentry over a vacant lot.

"You fucking bitch," Paige whispered and sunk to her knees.

Chapter Nine

"You're only taking my lower leg," Hal repeated and laughed, it caught in his throat and turned into a shriek.

He tried to sit up, but the restraints held his chest against the stretcher. He raised his head as high as his neck would allow and saw Lizzy draping restraints over his thighs. Before she had the chance to fasten them, Hal jack-knifed his unbroken leg and his knee hit her in the temple.

He heard the air puff out of her mouth before she stumbled and her hands flopped across his groin. He moved his wrist under the restraints and managed to grab a swatch of her hair. Lizzy made a guttural sound and stabbed her elbow down on his nuts. Pain seared up as if a live wire had been inserted in his abdomen. He gritted his teeth but held on.

He brought his knee up again and gave her another whack, this time on her cheek. He heard her grunt, the sound reminding him of an angry bull. All the while he was aware of a high-pitched bleating and his panicked mind wondered if a whole farmyard was loose in the house. The thought seemed so crazy, he almost laughed.

The struggle felt like it lasted for hours when, in fact, not even a minute passed. Lizzy put to bed any fight Hal had left when she raised her fist and slammed it down on his broken leg. He actually heard the bones crunch, it was a queer sound, like seashells rattling in a bucket. His vision blackened and his back arched. He let go of her hair as his whole body enveloped in a cold shaft of pain almost exquisite in its intensity.

He felt a vague awareness. First of restraints being pulled tight over his thighs and then his unbroken leg. Then, something hard being slid under his lower body. A thin leather strap was fastened around his thigh and pulled tight enough to cut into his flesh. He wanted to struggle, but the waves of pain still battered his lower body.

"Don't," he heard himself beg. "Don't cut me, *please*. Lizzy, please don't."

She made a clucking sound with her tongue and turned her back. He could still hear the bleating and then his gaze found the big, dark woman. She was flapping her hands near her head and staring at his legs.

"Please," he croaked. "Don't let her hurt me."

Soona's eyes flicked up and locked with his for less than a second before they drifted to the side. Hal saw the fear he felt reflected back at him.

Lizzy turned back holding a syringe. *She must have a lifetime supply of those things.* Tears streamed down his cheeks.

"Now, you're lucky I'm still going to give you this," she said and waved the needle. "After the way you attacked me, I should just do without the pain relief."

I bet you'd enjoy that, wouldn't you? You crazy bitch. "I'm sorry if I hurt you, but don't cut me. I'm begging you Lizzy, don't do this." He tried to sound calm and reasonable around his sobs.

"You'll thank me in the long run." She spoke in a distracted way, as if answering an inquisitive child.

She walked around the trolley and injected something into his leg. "That's a local," she said and tapped him on the calf. "Can you feel that?"

"Yes. Yes, I can. His words came out in a shaky whoosh.

She gave a little laugh and shook her head. Hal wished he was in on the joke because from his point of view there was nothing funny about what the looney with the needle planned to do. Even as he begged and cried, he could see she would complete the job she'd set out to do. Lizzy was one of those "always finish what you start" sort of girls. If she said she was going to cut your leg off, well, you'd better get yourself a good prosthetic because come hell or high water, your leg was coming off.

"Soona," Lizzy snapped. "Help me turn this trolley around. I want his leg near the instruments."

Soona's bleating quietened to weak mewling. She took the head of the trolley and spun it towards the door. Hal watched a large brown stain on the ceiling twirl and spotted a cobweb dangling from a bare bulb.

Lizzy picked up a large brown bottle and some gauze. A strong smell of iodine bathed the room, but Hal couldn't feel anything on his leg. *That's a good thing.* Then a feeling of complete understanding and utter terror. Not the horror movie kind, where the girl screams and covers her mouth, but the deep, bone-shaking punch-in-the-guts that steals your voice and loosens your bowls.

Lizzy moved back to the trolley, when she turned around she held the hacksaw. "That local I gave you will help, but," she paused. "I'm not gonna lie, it won't do a lot once I get down to the bone." The empty look in her eyes panicked him more than the evil looking hacksaw.

"N- N- No," Hal managed around chattering teeth. But Lizzy's head was already bent over his legs, her elbow moving back and forth.

Hal's eyes were wide, so wide it felt like they might burst from their sockets. He stared at the ceiling, focusing on the brown patch. He could hear a wet slopping sound and then a slow drip. His mind pulled him in all directions, but one insane thought kept circling, *she didn't even wash her fucking hands.*

When the hacksaw hit bone, all coherent thought ceased and Hal screamed. His screams piled on top of each other until blessed darkness rose up and took him.

Chapter Ten

A dark stain was all that remained of the snake. *The rest carried off by birds no doubt.* Paige ran the toe of her battered tennis shoe over the bloody mark – the only evidence that she and Hal had ever been there. The Silver Island Cheese factory loomed just as it had the day before, at odds with the bucolic setting.

Paige wandered over to the loading dock and sat down. She leaned back, her palms flat on the cool concrete, and stared at the spot where the Ford had been. It was easy to imagine Lizzy out here during the night, huffing and puffing, her large rear end pointing skywards while she fitted the spare tyre. At first, Paige had felt an overwhelming rage towards the woman, so much so she'd considered jogging back to the house and attacking her.

She'd even pictured the scene: she'd walk into the kitchen, pick up a pan, the heavy cast iron job she'd seen Lizzy use to fry eggs. *Eggs!* That got her blood boiling. She'd use a little trick Lizzy taught her and smack her in the forehead with the old pan. Bamb! But that had been half an hour ago and the energy that came with the rage quickly ebbed, leaving her exhausted and helpless.

Instead of swearing and imagining revenge scenarios, Paige tried to think through her options. She could try to walk back to the freeway or on to the roadhouse. If she had water, she could probably make it. *If I go slowly and stay on the road.* She looked down at her ankles, they were twice their normal size and an unhealthy scarlet.

"Bloody hell," she whispered, leaning forward and dropping her head into her hands. It was too far to go back, and too far to go forward. Where did that leave her? *Up shit creek.*

The light faded as dark shadows swallowed the carpark and loading bay. Paige checked the time. Four-thirty. She'd been gone for hours. She thought of Hal, probably waiting to hear the sound of approaching sirens coming to take him to hospital. Then inevitably, her thoughts turned to Lizzy. *Now what?* She most certainly would know Paige was gone. Would she do something to Hal? Paige pushed the thought from her mind. If she meant to hurt him, she wouldn't be trying so desperately to keep him alive.

The thought gave her some comfort. Lizzy had taken care of his wounds. She'd given him medication for the pain. Why would she do all that if she wanted to hurt him? Hurting Hal made no sense. She put her hand on her belly and stretched her back. Nothing about Lizzy's actions made sense but she couldn't take the chance that Hal might be in danger. She'd have to walk back to Mable House. *I'll find another way.*

Paige got to her feet and winced at the throbbing in her ankles. She looked around the carpark one last time as if hoping the Ford would magically appear. Then she headed for the road; it would be easier than going through the bush. She heard a kookaburra winding up into a full-blown laugh. As she headed back towards her captor, she was sure the bird was laughing at her.

Paige rounded the corner and walked along the turn-off for Mable House. Moving slowly, like an old lady, it took her twenty minutes to get even that far. The sound of her breathing came out loud and laboured, it filled her ears eclipsing all other noises. Not until the Holden bore down on her did she become aware of the rumbling engine.

The pale green ute veered over to the side of the road and came to a stop about ten meters ahead of Paige. She could see Lizzy in the cab, her broad shoulders hulking over the steering wheel. The woman made no move to get out.

* * *

The passenger door opened with a protesting squeal. Lizzy's eyes remained fixed ahead, she barely acknowledged Paige until the door closed behind her.

"Hal's taken a turn for the worse," she said, her bulbous grey eyes roving over Paige's face and body.

All the things Paige planned to say and do were forgotten. "What do you mean?" she asked, terrified of the answer.

Lizzy took her time. She crunched through the gears and performed a textbook three-point turn. "The bite was infected after all." She didn't look at Paige as she spoke, keeping her eyes on the road. "I did what I could to stabilise him."

When Paige heard herself speak, her voice sounded hoarse. "What do you mean stabilise?" *What have you done?*

Lizzy let out a long sigh as if Paige's questions were tiresome. "I've done what I can to combat the infection." She shrugged. "Now we'll just have to wait and see how he goes." Another pause. "Either he'll come good or he won't."

Paige closed her eyes and balled her fingers into fists. She knew she shouldn't antagonise the woman, provoking her would only put her and Hal in a worse position. But she had to ask. Whatever the outcome, at least there'd be no more pretending.

"Drive me to the roadhouse?" Paige asked, her tone flat and truculent.

For the first time since she'd mentioned Hal, Lizzy looked over at her. The look in her eyes made Paige's skin crawl; a look of sly pleasure. Paige got the feeling she had finally got a good look at the real Lizzy Hatcher.

"Let's just worry about one thing at a time," Lizzy said, and looked back at the road.

* * *

This time, Lizzy parked the ute around the rear of the house, near the ramshackle outbuildings. As soon as the vehicle stopped, Paige sprang out of the cab and headed towards the back door. She could hear the woman behind her slamming the driver's door. Paige wondered if Lizzy would try to stop her entering the house or seeing Hal. If she did, then Paige decided, she'd hit the woman in the head with the frying pan. She'd do whatever it took to get to Hal.

To Paige's surprise, Lizzy didn't seem to be following her. When Paige entered the kitchen, she paused and looked back through the screen door. Lizzy headed away from the house and towards the sheds.

Paige wanted to rush through the drawing room and up the stairs, but she made herself stop at the sink. She forced herself to slow down and think of the baby. She felt a wave of light-headedness and knew she couldn't go much longer without a drink. Paige grabbed a glass from the draining board and filled it under the tap. The water was tepid, but it tasted wonderful to her parched throat. *Next time I'll take water.* The thought took her by surprise. She refilled the glass and nodded to herself. *Yes, there will be a next time. I'll find a way to get us out of this mess.*

* * *

When Paige reached Hal's room, the door was closed and the air on the third floor redolent with an unpleasant smell. Paige couldn't place it — somehow heavy and metallic at the same time. It put her teeth on edge and made her uneasy. She rubbed her damp palm on the front of her dress and grabbed the battered brass knob.

The first thing that struck her was Hal's breathing; it sounded deep and even, as though he were asleep. The sun had disappeared and darkness blanketed the house. Without turning on the light, it was difficult to make out his face. She grabbed the phone from her bra and switched on the light. A cloud of soft blue illuminated the bed. Hal's eyes were closed and his mouth slightly open.

Paige took a step closer and sat down beside him. She put her hand on his brow to feel for a fever and was alarmed by how cool he felt. She noticed the tube running from his arm up to the drip and wondered if Lizzy was giving him antibiotics. In the glow of the phone light, his skin looked strange, almost bleached of colour. Paige leaned closer and put her cheek against his.

She felt the need to be close to him so strongly it almost overwhelmed her. Since this nightmare began, it seemed like something had yanked him away from her by forces beyond her control. Even now, he seemed changed, as if something about him had been snatched away.

Hal moaned softly in his sleep, his breath warm on her cheek. Paige pulled back and looked into his face, he grimaced in pain. He didn't have a fever; his skin was too cool. If his bite were infected, surely he'd be hot? She wondered about the pain. *It must be his broken leg.*

She ran her hand over his arm and leaned forward so she could kiss the tattoo on his inner wrist. His skin felt icy, his pulse thin and distant. Something touched the back of her head and she looked up startled.

Hal's eyes were open and his right hand gently touched her hair. His green eyes were red-rimmed and raw. She thought they were watering, but when a tear ran down his cheek, she realised he was crying.

"I'm sorry," she said. "The car was gone, I had to come back."

Hal nodded, but he didn't seem to be hearing her. "Paige," he whispered. "She took my leg." His voice trembled so violently she wasn't sure she'd heard him right.

Paige wrapped her fingers around his hand. "What, Hal? What did she do?"

"She cut off my leg," his voice louder now and filled with anguish. His grip on her hand tightened. "She cut off my leg," he repeated it as if he couldn't believe his own words.

Paige shook her head and opened her mouth to speak, but nothing came out. She could see the truth in Hal's raw, haunted eyes. Her gaze travelled down the bed and by the faint blue glow of the phone, she saw the depression in the sheet at the end of his left leg.

"No. Oh no. No, no." The words tumbled out. Paige could see the evidence with her own eyes. She could hear the jagged horror in Hal's voice, but couldn't take it in.

Her mind kept coming back to the smell; she realised that when she'd come up the stairs, she'd smelt blood. Hal's blood. *This is my fault. I did this to him.* She'd left him alone with a mad woman who'd punished him for Paige's attempted escape. She had no doubt Lizzy amputated Hal's healthy leg to punish her.

She put her head on Hal's chest and felt him wrap his arms around her. She wished she were strong enough to pick him up and carry him out of this house of horrors. She could feel him sobbing into her neck, as his arms clung to her like a drowning man.

"I'm sorry, Hal. I'm so sorry," she whispered, but no amount of regret would undo what Lizzy had done to him. An image of Hal kicking a soccer ball on the beach in Bali flashed in her mind. They were on their honeymoon; he wore dark blue board-shorts and a straw trilby. He'd started kicking the ball with some local kids and pretty soon they had a game going. In her mind, she could see him, tanned and healthy, smiling at her as she watched him play.

She stayed in his arms sobbing for a few minutes, but as strong emotions do, her grief faltered. Her mind kicked in. Fury took hold, racing through her like poison. She wanted to punish Lizzy, hurt her the way she'd hurt Hal. But then another thought crept in, *why?* Why was it so important to her that they stay?

She pulled back and took Hal's face in her hands. "Tell me what happened?"

She could see Hal battling to get himself under control; her heart went out to him. She wanted to take his pain away and give him comfort, but right now she had to work out what Lizzy wanted from them.

"She came in and asked where you were." Hal dragged his forearm over his eyes and took a shuddering breath. "She didn't even give me time to answer. She told the other one," he frowned.

"Soona?" Paige offered.

"Yeah. She told her to help and they put me on a trolley." He gave a humourless smile. "I tried to fight her off, but she grabbed my leg."

Paige listen as Hal recounted the story. There were times when he struggled to speak, moments when Paige wished she could cover her ears and turn away, but she wouldn't allow herself that mercy. She needed to hear what he had gone through. She had to know what Lizzy was capable of.

When he finished, Paige kissed him on the mouth. His lips were cool and she could feel a tremor in him that ran through his entire body and out his mouth. She guessed he was in shock and wondered how hard it would be for him when this nightmare ended and they were back in the real world. *If we get back to the real world.*

"I'm going to get us out of here." It came out with more strength and conviction than she felt.

"No," Hal said. "I want you to go as soon as you get the chance. But this time, don't come back."

"I'm not leaving you again …"

"You and the baby come first," he said gripping her arm. "Get as far away from here as you can. Do it as soon as you can."

Paige wanted to argue, but the exhausted look on his haggard face made her hold her tongue. "Okay, but let's wait a few days." She could see him ready to protest so she spoke quickly. "Just long enough for her to drop her guard, and to give me time to plan how I'm going to do it." *And for me to make sure you come back from this.*

"Okay," he said and closed his eyes.

Paige leaned her head on the bed and listened to his breathing, at first shallow and then gradually deepening. When she was sure he slept, she turned off her phone light and sat in the darkness watching his outline, listening to him moaning in his sleep.

* * *

Things moved slowly over the next two days. If Lizzy had expected anger and recriminations, Paige didn't give them to her. She kept her emotions guarded. After the night she found out about Hal's leg, she only spoke of what happened once – thanking Lizzy for saving her husband's life. Lizzy responded by reminding her that Mable House wasn't a resort and she should be doing more to help.

Paige took over Hal's care, making sure she was the one to feed and wash him. The thought of Lizzy touching him any more than necessary made Paige's skin crawl. Hal slept a lot, whether his body needed it or so his mind could escape from what had been done to him, she wasn't sure. If it were the latter, she couldn't blame him for needing to shut out the horror. But he seemed to be drifting away from her and a selfish part wanted him to snap back and solve all their problems.

For her part, Paige busied herself quietly watching Lizzy, taking careful note of the woman's timetable: when she woke up, when she ate, and most importantly, when she slept. Convinced Lizzy had taken the Ford, Paige hoped she might glean information about where it might be hidden.

* * *

On the morning of the fourth day at Mable House, Lizzy sat at the kitchen table drinking a cup of milky tea laced with two heaped spoons of sugar. She wore another one of her patented navy shirt and pants outfits. Occasionally licking her thick, blunt index finger she flicked through the pages of an ancient copy of Gardening Australia. *She wrapped those thick fingers around a hacksaw and cut off Hal's leg,* Paige thought and a sob lodged in her throat.

"I think we'll have marron for tea tonight," Lizzy said to no one in particular.

It was early, a little past seven in the morning. The three women sat at the kitchen table; Soona champed her way through three slices of thick, toasted bread and jam, eyes dreamy and unfocused, while Paige drank a cup of strong tea and tried to force down a slice of toast. She'd come to realise that meals, à la Lizzy were plain and stodgy, consisting of generous servings of boiled potatoes, fried sausages or chops and homemade bread, usually washed down with tea or fresh lemonade.

"Marron," Paige said, her tone casually interested. She was getting good at playing the, *I've no interest in leaving* and *I'm so grateful* game.

Lizzy lifted a surprisingly delicate china cup to her mouth and drank the last of her tea before she answered. "We've got a dam." She put her cup down and stood. "After Soona's finished her jobs, she can take you out and show you." She turned to Soona and said, "Take her and show her the dam. Don't touch the cages." She spoke in a loud, slow voice and waited for Soona to answer.

"Marron," Soona said. It was the first word Paige had heard her speak. Up until that moment, she'd assumed Soona was completely non-verbal.

"Yes," Lizzy nodded. "That's right."

Lizzy headed for the drawing room and then Paige heard her heavy tread ascend the stairs. *Making her morning rounds in an almost empty hospital,* Paige thought grimly. She'd already been in and given Hal breakfast; a scrambled egg and a slice of toast; he'd eaten reluctantly, with the sort of grim resignation of a prize fighter trying to bulk up in time for the big night.

Paige listened to Lizzy's thumping footfalls climb the stairs. She was eager to get a better look around the property, and discovering Soona's limited language skills gave her an idea. As soon as she was sure Lizzy was out of earshot, Paige turned to Soona, who now stood at the sink washing the breakfast dishes. She watched the other woman for a moment. She wore dark denim jeans, the seat faded to a threadbare white. A brown checked shirt strained over slumped shoulders.

"Do you like cola?" Paige asked.

Soona's arms continued to move working on the dishes, but she made no reply. Paige picked up her cup and plate and walked over to the sink. "Do you like cola?" she asked again.

"Cola," Soona said. And took the plate and cup from Paige without looking at her.

"When we go to get see the crayfish, I'll give you some cola if you take me to my car," Paige said softly. I need to get some clean clothes, that's all."

After a moment, Soona repeated the word, "cola."

"Yes," Paige said. "But don't tell anyone, cola's bad for your teeth."

A short time later, Paige followed Soona through the garden; they passed the Hills Hoist ducking to avoid flapping wet sheets. Soona led her through a human-sized hole in a clump of grevillea bushes to a section of the property that was home to a large vegetable patch. Paige had never been this far behind the house and found herself amazed by the way the property seemed to go on and on:

sheds, led to veggie patches, which in turn led to a small paddock.

The smell of damp grass and manure floated on the morning air. Two cows, one a soft chocolate brown, the other black with a patch of white on its hindquarters were intent on grazing and ignored them as they passed. The layout of the property seemed helter-skelter, nothing really made sense in terms of function, but Paige reminded herself, *this crazy maze is Lizzy's kingdom.*

Once they were past the paddock, Soona grunted her way over a small upsurge. At the top of the rise, a gully dam came into view. The setting, so idyllic that, for a moment, Paige felt awed by its perfection. The natural dip in the landscape was clothed in lush green grass. On the right side a sandy bank led to a small bleached wood jetty. On the other side, an ancient gum curved towards the water as if stooping to drink. The sunlight glittered across the surface of the dam casting the whole scene in a yellow glow.

Before they descended the slope, Paige touched Soona's arm. The woman shuffled out of reach and stopped. "Before we go down there," Paige said. "Let's go to my car and get the cola."

Soona swayed from side to side, her head bobbing up and down. She seemed to be caught between action and understanding.

"You like cola," Paige tried again. "Take me to my car and we can have some." When Soona remained silent, Paige tried another approach. "Would you like me to tell you a story?"

Soona started to sit down on the grassy slope. "No, not yet. The car first, then cola and a story. Okay?" Paige forced the urgency out of her voice.

"Okay," Soona said, her eyes fixed on something only she could see in the distance.

Paige felt a flutter of excitement and her mind lurched forward. The car was her best chance of escape, if it was drivable there was nothing to stop her leaving immediately. She doubted Soona would try to stop her, but if she did … Paige's thoughts faltered. *If she tries to stop me, I'll do whatever I have to.* The coldness of her thoughts surprised her, as if they came from a place in her she didn't know existed. A dark place. A primordial place that housed a part of her very different to the Paige the parents who met with her to discuss their children saw. This voice, Paige realised, came from a cold, hard woman, who'd stop at nothing to protect what was hers.

Soona turned away from the dam and plodded back towards the paddock. She moved with a side to side gait that made her look like an overgrown toddler. Paige was using her, she knew that. Taking advantage of the woman's childlike trust was easier than she wanted to acknowledge, something she didn't care to dwell on. Getting to the car was all that mattered.

Paige followed her, glancing over her shoulder expecting Lizzy to leap out from behind a bush or materialise in the veggie patch. Soona moved towards the paddock and the ground became marshy. Soft earth sucked at Paige's shoes making each step more difficult. Soona seemed unhindered by the sludge, lifting her knees high and taking great loping steps around the wire fence.

By the time they reached the barn, Paige's tennis shoes and ankles were thick with mud and she panted from exhaustion. At first it seemed they headed for the barn, but then Soona continued on behind the building and towards what looked like a disused dirt track.

Paige could feel a stitch gripping her right side. She put her hands on her hips and stopped. "Soona, wait. I have to stop for a minute."

Soona wandered back towards the paddock and ducked under the fence. She ambled over to the chocolate coloured cow. It raised its head and regarded her with big soft eyes and a wet puff of its cavernous nostrils. Soona reached into the front pocket of her jeans and produced a stump of carrot. The cow, unfazed by her presence, familiar with the routine, strolled towards her, head up and belly swinging. Paige watched the woman hold out her hand and let the cow gobble the chunk of carrot. Soona patted the animal between the ears and in return it gave a contented snort.

For the first time since the idea of using Soona occurred to her, Paige considered what Lizzy might do to the woman when she found out she'd helped Paige escape. She'd been so focused on manipulating Soona, she'd almost stopped thinking of her as human. That shameful realisation made her cringe inwardly at her own callousness. She knitted her fingers together and brought them up to her mouth. *I don't have a choice. She'll be okay. Lizzy won't hurt her.* And then out of that dark place, the one that seemed to be getting bigger all the time, *she's not my problem.* In her head, the voice sounded flat and emotionless.

"Soona, let's go." When Soona looked up, Paige smiled and gave a little wave.

The dirt road consisted of little more than a four-metre-wide trail through the bush. The path was topped with a carpet of fallen twigs, seedpods and weeds. Sunlight struggled to penetrate the thick canopy casting thin shafts of light along the track. The air felt cooler, the sweat that had been gathering on Paige's brow ran down her face in icy drips. They'd only taken a few steps and already the bush seemed to be closing around them, pulling at her clothes and blocking off all sound from the outside world.

So isolated and well-covered was the track, without Soona's help, Paige doubted she'd have ever found it on her own. She had to hand it to Lizzy, she certainly knew how to hide something, even something as big as a car. No sooner had the word popped into Paige's head than something glinted ahead and to the left.

The Ford was parked on the edge of the track in an area that widened into a clearing. It sat like a huge, orange insect draped haphazardly in fallen gum and tuart branches. Lizzy had obviously thought no one would ever find it, the branches were barely covering the bonnet with one or two scattered on the roof.

Paige let out a laugh that turned into a whoop and darted forward. Finding the car was the first thing that had gone right since the snake bite four days ago. She trailed her hand along the vehicle, pulling branches free and dropping them on the ground. The flat had been changed, making the vehicle drivable again. A flutter of excitement in her stomach grew until her hands shook. If the keys were in the ignition, nothing could stop her.

She licked her lips and opened the driver's side door. The inside of the car smelled of pine air freshener and something else. Paige took a deep breath and thought she caught a whiff of Hal's cologne. The smile that blossomed on her face vanished.

There were no keys in the ignition.

Her excitement waned but didn't die. When they set off on holiday, Hal took the spare from the kitchen and put it in his suitcase. Paige dashed to the back of the vehicle and opened the hatch. The two suitcases were gone. She ran her hands through her stringy, unwashed hair and closed her eyes. *Why would she take our suitcases?*

Paige turned around and leaned her butt against the open back of the Ford. The missing keys were a setback, but the game wasn't over yet. She knew where the car was, all she had to do was find the keys.

"It's doable," the words slipped out of her mouth, the confidence in her voice sounded like it had come from someone else. "Let's get you your cola," she said to Soona who was bending to pick a bunch of stinkweed.

* * *

They made their way back to the dam; this time Paige took the lead and Soona followed behind. Even after the march around the muddy paddock, Paige felt invigorated, as if seeing the Ford worked to remind her that the world still existed beyond Mable House. For a few days, that had been a bit cloudy for her and probably more so for Hal.

She climbed the upswing that led to the dam, when she reached the top, she glanced over her shoulder at the grevillea bushes, their spidery white flowers shivered in the breeze. Paige turned and headed down the slope, the perfection of the gully dam now lost on her. She moved swiftly, they'd been away from the house for too long already, if Lizzy realised they'd been up to something there was no telling what she might do.

Paige plopped down onto the grass and pulled off her shoes. The muscles in the back of her calves, already complaining over the march through the mud, groaned. Her ankles were mottled with insect bites and stained with mud; her knees scabbed from kneeling in the carpark when Hal was hurt. She scratched at her ankles and watched Soona walk out onto the short jetty still clutching the bunch of stink weeds. Paige felt a sudden wave of affection for the woman and quickly looked away. She couldn't afford to let anything distract her from what she had to do. Becoming fond of Soona would only make things more difficult.

Paige clamoured to her feet and walked across the sandy bank into the water. She let out a sigh as the cool liquid lapped at her calves and soothed the itching of the bites. The water around her legs grew cloudy with mud. She bent and rinsed her shoes, using her thumb to rub away the worst of the stains.

When she straightened up, she noticed thin ropes running from the jetty out across the water and then disappearing. She turned and tossed her shoes onto the bank and then waded over to the jetty. She grabbed one of the ropes, it felt slimy from years in and out of the water. Yanking on it, she could feel something heavy move under the water. She guessed it was a marron trap.

"Don't touch. Don't touch," Soona repeated over and over in a monotone voice.

"It's alright, sweetheart, I just want to look. I'll put it back." Paige wasn't sure why she wanted to see the trap. Maybe because, like everything else here, it was hidden and she was tired of not knowing what was going on under the surface.

The trap felt surprisingly weighty, she bent her knees and pulled one arm over the other. *You'll feel that later*, she warned herself, but she couldn't seem to stop. The edge of the cage broke the surface about four metres away and then disappeared back under the water. Paige heaved the rope through her arms and could feel the cage bobbing along the sandy bottom.

Still standing in the water, she gave the rope a final yank and the bars of the cage wavered into view under the clear, yellow water. She spotted the crayfish at once. There were at least four of them, large and black as night. They were clustered around something at the bottom of the cage. Paige wondered if it was some sort of bait and leaned over to get a better look.

"Don't touch. Don't touch," Soona's voice shrilled from the jetty.

"I'm not going to touch it," Paige said and took a step deeper into the dam.

Feeling the movement of the water, the marron skittered around the cage, the bait now abandoned as they tried to escape. Paige blinked and leaned over the water. The shape at the bottom of the cage was irregular and white. She squinted and shifted to the left a little to get a better angle on what she was looking at.

The shape coalesced into clarity. Paige's stomach clenched and an ugly shriek flew out of her mouth. A foot. A human foot with a large metal hook running through it. Paige jammed the heel of her hand in her mouth and bit down. She could see thin, white ribbons of flesh streaming from the severed limb.

She dropped the rope and staggered backwards, her feet scrambling for purchase on the sandy bottom. She screamed, hearing herself make the noise but unaware of doing it. Water thumped around her as she turned and scampered onto the bank. Her heart hammered in her ears, and her limbs shook.

She made it as far as the grassy incline and dropped to one knee. All the excitement at finding the car, the sense of hope she'd felt, vanished. She closed her eyes. All she could see were those ribbons of flesh waving in the yellow water. Her stomach contracted and a jet of hot fluid sprayed out of her mouth, puddling on the grass.

For a few minutes, she stared at the pool of partially digested food, her vision obscured by watery eyes. When the foul slick came back into view, Paige stood and dragged her arm across her mouth. *We're going to die here.* Another sob burst through her lips.

Any illusions she'd had about Lizzy and what she might be capable of were gone. The woman was sick. An evil creature. And now, Paige couldn't pretend she had things under control. Things were so far out of control that the world spun.

Keep it together, keep it together, she repeated the words in her mind like some sort of self-help mantra. She needed to stay calm and find the keys. If she could do that, then maybe they had a chance of getting out of Mable House. She had to play the game a little longer. Could she do it after what she'd just seen? She didn't know, but she'd soon find out.

Paige's bare feet slid on the cool grass. She realised she'd left her shoes at the dam. If she had any hope of escaping, she'd need them. It would mean going back to the dam. Seeing the cages again. Even if she couldn't see the severed foot with the undulating ribbons of flesh, she'd know it was there, just below the surface. She paused near the opening in the grevillea bush and looked back towards the rolling incline. Soona made her way over the rise clutching Paige's shoes.

She watched the woman amble towards her holding out the sneakers and another wave of affection washed over her. This time it came wrapped up with gratitude. For the moment, the dark voice remained silent. She suspected Soona knew and understood a great deal more about what was going on here than Paige had given her credit for.

"Thank you, Soona. It's very kind of you to bring me my shoes," she said and reached out a shaky hand.

The baby, possibly upset by Paige's fierce rush of emotions at the dam, shifted and kicked. Paige took the shoes and put her free hand on her belly, gently patting the stirring baby. She wondered what all this was doing to her unborn child. She'd read somewhere, possibly in one of the dozens of pregnancy books she'd read, that mothers can communicate stress to their babies.

Noticing Soona's eyes on her abdomen, Paige reached out her hand. "Do you want to feel my baby?" she asked.

Soona's eyes flicked between Paige's hand and her belly. Then, maybe deciding that feeling the baby was worth enduring being touched, Soona reached out her hand. Paige guided it to her belly, carefully, not wanting to overwhelm the woman with her contact. Paige put the woman's hand on her stomach and within a second, the baby shifted.

Soona chuckled, a hearty infectious sound. In spite of all the horror, Paige found herself chuckling along with her.

"Paige's baby," she said.

"Lizzy's baby," Soona said, still pressing her hand against Paige's belly.

Paige gave a nervous laugh. "No, sweetheart. This is Paige's baby." *Not everything here belongs to Lizzy.*

"Lizzy's baby," Soona said again.

Paige wanted to explain to her that the baby was in her tummy, so it was hers, when the words died in her mouth. Like being hit by lightning, realisation dawned on her. The reason they were here; why Hal was immobilised upstairs.

None of this had ever been about him *or* her. They were just a means to an end. *It's the baby.* The moment Lizzy saw her in the road, their fate had been sealed.

Chapter Eleven

Hal had come to recognise Lizzy's footsteps – a dull thump as the woman hammered down her heels with every step. Even the sound of her set his nerves jangling and his heart thumping. Each time she approached the room, his heart raced and his mind screamed at the possibility that she'd come to do him more harm.

"How are you feeling today?" Lizzy asked from the doorway.

She asked the same question every day, most times not waiting for an answer. How he felt or didn't feel was of no real interest to Lizzy Hatcher. She'd made her indifference clear enough when she tied him down and sawed off his leg. But more than the cruelty, the flat disinterested look in her ghostly eyes told him all he needed to know. He was no more present in her world than a feeder fish to a shark.

"I'm doing just fine," Hal said and turned his head towards the small window.

He couldn't see much of the outside world, just a rectangle of blue and a long slash of sunlight on the worn floorboards. He thought of turning his face up to the sun and closing his eyes and tried to imagine the golden light against his eyelids.

"Your stump *is* healing nicely. Good thing I got to it in time." She pushed her ever-present trolley over to the bed, pulled back the sheet and leaned over his legs.

He watched the crown of her head, hovering just over his knees. Her scalp, shiny and pink with flecks of dandruff. He could smell lemons and something like spoiled milk.

"You know, Hal, when Mable House was first built in 1928, it was a workhouse for young women who found themselves in trouble." She pulled the dressing off the wound on his broken leg. While he'd been unconscious, she taken the liberty of stitching up the gash made by the Ford's rim.

Hal fought back a groan and clenched his teeth. He could feel sweat running down his cheeks. Changing his bandages and dressings was the most painful part of each agonising day.

"That's what they called it back then." She straightened up and made her fingers into quotation marks. "'In trouble.' A funny way of saying pregnant, but that's what they called it."

Hal wasn't sure where her story was going or if he should say something, so he just nodded.

"A lot of desperate young woman had their babies in this house. A lot of frightened girls ..." her voice trailed off and for a moment she just stared at him.

She lapsed into silence for a while, the only sounds her breathing and the sharp rip of surgical tape.

"After the war, Mable House became a hospital for returning soldiers. Men who didn't have anyone to care for them. Men like you."

Hal was taken aback. "What do you mean like me?" The words were out before he could stop himself. He'd promised Paige he wouldn't do anything to provoke the woman. He thought of the way she'd fought him, twisted his broken leg, tied him down and quickly added, "I mean, like me in what way?"

93

"Amputees. Or," she nodded to his leg. "Men with infections that ended up losing limbs." She finished replacing the dressing and moved around to the other side of the bed. "Do you want something for the pain before I start on your stump?" she asked, almost kindly.

Yes, he did want something for the pain. He wanted it very badly. Bellow his knees lay a road map of searing agony, and when she changed the bandage on his stump, he felt like his flesh and bone were being shredded by meat hooks.

"A couple of paracetamol would help," he said and tried for a grateful smile.

Lizzy shrugged and went to the cupboard and got the tablets. She put them in the palm of his hand and then handed him a glass of water.

"That's when my father came to Mable House," she continued with her story. "He was a doctor and he came to help the wounded servicemen. A great man." Hal noticed that the tone of her voice changed when she talked about the house; and when she mentioned her father, her face flushed with pleasure. He didn't know if the improvement in her mood was good or bad so he said nothing.

Lizzy re-dressed his severed leg. When she touched the bulky bandages, sheets of pain washed over him. Lizzy seemed oblivious to his gritted teeth and sweat-soaked face.

"My father helped hundreds of people over the years," Lizzy continued. "After the soldiers, the girls came again." She shrugged. "In the sixties, there were no shortage of girls in a jam. My father helped the girls too." Her tone changed. The faraway wistful look, that softened her features, vanished and something darker clouded her face. "Girls like your wife, about to drop and running all over the countryside in a mini skirt." She gave him a pointed look, heavy with disapproval.

"My wife," Hal said, around shallow breaths, "isn't in a jam. We're married and looking forward to having a child."

He tried to keep his tone mild, but the smug look on her face was almost more than he could bear.

Lizzy's protruding grey eyes looked shiny, glassy like they'd been polished in a shop and pushed into her sockets by a giant doll maker. "Maybe once, but now she's saddled with a cripple and has a baby on the way; that sounds like a jam, don't you think?"

Hal swallowed and clenched the edges of the bed. His stump screamed as though shards of glass swam below the skin. Lizzy's change of mood was terrifying in its swiftness. But the word *cripple* really hit home. His stomach felt hollow and the strength left his arms. He wanted her to finish and leave him in peace so he could stare at the window and image a time when Paige and he would spend whole afternoons in bed. A time when his world wasn't full of pain.

"Alright," Lizzy said. "All done." She flipped the sheet back up and walked briskly out of the room.

Hal let out his breath and his whole body shuddered. He could hear her somewhere close by running water and clanking instruments. *The worst of it is over*, he told himself and tried to catch his breath. With a tremendous effort, he focused his mind on something other than his legs. The things Lizzy had said; he wondered what it was all about. His thinking felt so scattered, concentrating and following a thought seemed almost impossible. But his instincts told him it was important. Some of it seemed to be desultory rambling, some downright cruel, but he was beginning to understand Lizzy well enough to know that nothing she did or said was truly random. *So what was she trying to tell him?*

She bustled back into the room and snatched up the jug from the locker. A few moments later she returned with it freshly filled. "Having you here is a lot of work for me," she said and set the jug down hard enough to rattle the locker and make the water slosh noisily over the rim.

Hal tried to think of something to say that would calm her mood. "I'm grateful to you for taking such good care of me." He hoped he sounded more sincere than he felt.

For a moment, she stared at the water and didn't reply. Hal eyed the jug and wondered if he could reach it in time to smash it over her head. He could see himself driving the jug into her scalp, smashing bone and shredding skin. He'd never hit a woman in his life. Hell, a week ago he would've said he never would, but the thought of hurting Lizzy became more and more appealing.

"I bet you think that pretty-boy face of yours is really charming." She pulled her attention away from the jug. "But it doesn't matter."

The finality in her words that chilled him. *She's never going to let us go.* "I mean it," he added quickly and then before he could stop himself, "When we leave, I'll be sure to tell people how much you've done for us."

"Hal, I may be a country girl, but I'm not stupid and neither are you." She seemed to be about to say more, but stopped. Her eyes narrowed and flitted to the window.

Hal followed her gaze; he could see nothing of interest on the grimy glass. Then he heard it, the sound that grabbed her attention. At first he thought there was a fly in the room, buzzing around the pane, but then it grew louder, deeper. He watched her rush to the window, rubber soles thumping on the boards. The casual confidence of her usual movements replaced by a hurried urgency.

"Is that a ..."

"Shut-up," she snapped, and flew from the room, the door crashing shut behind her.

The buzzing turned into a rumble that stuttered and coughed. There was no mistaking the sound of a motorbike. Hal pushed himself up in the bed, in a moment of madness, he almost swung his legs over the side before they protested with shrieks of pain.

96

He pushed out a fevered breath and looked around the room, searching for what, he didn't know. He had to get out of bed, if he could make it to the window, he might be able to call for help. The sound of gravel spraying and tyres crunching sprang up from the front of the house. Hal slid his butt to the left side of the bed and flipped back the sheets. Lizzy had flown from the room in such a hurry, she'd left her trolley behind. If he could put some weight on his broken leg, he might be able to lean his body over the trolley and wheel over to the window.

He used his arms to lift himself closer to the edge of the bed. Balancing like a gymnast on the vaulting horse, he focused on keeping his legs straight out in front of him. Outside, the motorbike hiccupped then abruptly stopped. Someone had arrived at Mable House and judging by the way Lizzy pegged out of the room, the visitor was unexpected.

Hal reached out and for one breath-taking second, he almost hit the trolley away from the bed. He snapped his wrist up and latched onto the edge before it could spin out of reach. When he had it firmly in his grasp, he bent his elbow and pulled it alongside the bed.

A door banged open and then slammed shut somewhere below. *Is someone in the house?* He didn't think so. His money was on Lizzy rushing outside. As if to confirm his suspicions, voices echoed below the window. He couldn't make out what they were saying, but the deep quality of some of the sounds, told him that one was male.

He lifted the remnants of left of his left leg to the side of the bed and began lowering it. The pain flared, but not unbearably. Salty sweat ran down his forehead and dripped into his eyes. He used his forearm to wipe it away and then picked up his broken leg, holding it just above the ankle, he moved it to the side of the bed.

A shaft of agony ran the length of his leg. His foot, the size of a small melon and roughly the colour of the grape jelly his mother used to make, twitched. He swore and froze with his leg grasped in both hands, suspended in mid-air. He panted like a dog on a hot day and lowered the leg back onto the bed. His heart beat so fast he could hear the blood whooshing in his ears. He allowed himself five seconds to gather courage and lifted his leg again.

When he swung his broken leg over the side of the bed, the world shifted and his vision clouded until the room swam in soupy fog. The swarming razor blades attacked in full force under his skin.

"I'm coming you saw-happy bitch. Get ready for the cripple," he spat the words out through clenched teeth and took hold of the trolley with both hands.

When he had it in position, he used his forearm to sweep the tape, scissors and various other paraphernalia from the top. An assortment of items clattered and rolled across the floor. This was it, time to find out if his foot could take some weight long enough to bend his body over the ancient trolley.

He could still hear voices, faint but clearly coming from below the window. It might have been a change in the wind, but Hal was sure whoever the voice belonged to, was getting agitated. Then an unmistakable shout. The words *Jesus* and *what* rang out in a deep male voice, clear as day.

If Lizzy was out there, she'd be trying to get rid of her visitor. The faceless man might be getting back on his bike right now. If Hal didn't make himself move, the man might be gone before he got halfway across the room. He put his foot to the floor, and felt the roughness of warn boards under his toes. He leaned forward and pressed down slightly. The pain, so sudden and fierce jolted him back, his ass nearly slipping off the bed.

Tears sprang into his eyes. He hung his head and watched his chest heaving up and down. He couldn't make himself stand. His mind wanted to, he could even see himself rolling across the floor on the trolley like a child body-surfing through the shallows, but he couldn't make that final move. He shook his head and droplets of sweat splattered the trolley. He let go of the metal sides and rubbed his sweaty palms on his pyjama shirt.

Okay. You've been laying in that bed blubbering and dreaming about times gone by for days, time to act or time to die. He gripped the side of the trolley and pushed down on his toes. His leg, still throbbing from his last attempt, exploded into a million bursts of agony. He pushed forward and felt his butt leave the bed.

Tendons sprung out on his neck, and the room echoed with his own hoarse gasping. With a final push, he lunged forward, eyes that only a few days ago twinkled over the top of his sunglasses were now wide and red rimmed. For a moment he remained balanced on the trolley, slumped over on his stomach with one foot barely grazing the floor. He would have to use his foot like he was riding a scooter if he had any hope of reaching the window. He put the ball of his foot on the floor, it felt numb from the swelling. *Numb is good*, he thought. *The less I can feel, the better.*

"This is it," he said aloud and pushed down.

He let out a bellow that filled the room and the trolley rolled forward. The window grew larger, a few more pushes and he'd reach it. Sweat trickled from his hair and spattered onto the dusty boards. He paused to listen, terrified that he'd hear the sound of the motorbike's engine revving to life. That's when it came – shrill and urgent, but unmistakably Paige's voice.

Hearing her terror got him moving. He pushed off with his toes, whether his frantic need to help his wife overrode the pain or the agony had in fact lessened, he didn't know, but this time the pain neared bearable. One more push and he'd be at the window. Then the world exploded.

Chapter Twelve

Paige strode towards the rickety steps leading to the back door. If she had to hazard a guess, she'd say the keys were somewhere in Lizzy and Soona's living quarters. That was as good a place as any to start looking. She grabbed the splintered wood banister and started up. It took her a few seconds to realise something wasn't right.

She stopped, one foot resting on the veranda, head turned to the side. The sound came again, *voices*. A man's voice punched the air followed by what Paige recognised as Lizzy speaking rapidly. Their conversation floated around the house, carried on the morning breeze.

Paige backed down the steps. She clasped her damp shoes to her chest and followed the sound towards the front of the house. Her heart fluttered in her throat and her mouth suddenly went dry. She padded along the broken stone path that led to the corner of the building and stopped.

"You said the eighth and today's the eighth," the man said with an edge of impatience.

Paige reached out her hand and touched the side of the building, the crumbling cement felt chalky on her fingertips. A million what-ifs spun in her mind. What if he was Lizzy's husband and they were in on this together? What if he's dangerous? She recalled asking herself the very same question when Lizzy first stopped on the road; if she'd been more cautious, maybe they wouldn't be in this mess.

"I'm sorry, Wade. It's just not convenient today. Come back on the eighth of next month and you can start then." Lizzy's tone had a rushed urgency and for the first time since Paige met the woman, she sounded frazzled.

Paige decided she'd heard enough. Clearly, Lizzy wanted to get rid of the man. If he played any part in the woman's crazy plan, why would she be trying to get rid of him? Paige pushed herself away from the house and jogged towards the voices. She could hear the exchange of words continue.

"I've got another job next month and I turned down work at Holdridge's place in Mount Barker to fit you in," the man's voice rose a notch, not quite angry, but getting there. "If you want those trees cleared before summer, it has to be now."

"I told you, I'm sorry. What more do you want?" Lizzy's voice bordered on shrill.

"The only reason I drove all the way out here was because your father was so good to my Aunty Maude. He never would have mucked me about like this."

Paige rounded the corner. The man glanced at her then did a double take. His mouth dropped open.

"Jesus, Lizzy. What's going on?" he asked, looking from Paige to Lizzy with wide eyes.

Paige saw the look on the man's face and realised how shocking she must appear: her hair clung to her head in dirty clumps, her dress torn, covered in mud and grass stains, and her legs scraped and cut. She stumbled forward, trying to form words, but could only produce a series of rasping sobs.

The man Lizzy had called Wade looked like a skinny, elderly biker. His big droopy moustache worked up and down as he spoke.

"What's happened? Is this why you're trying to get rid of me?"

Before Lizzy could answer, Paige seized the man by the front of his black AC/DC shirt, her fingers digging into his chest hard enough to make him cry out and grab her around the wrists.

"Settle down and tell me what's going on," he said, looking down into Paige's desperate face.

The dryness that had started in Paige's mouth now spread to her throat. "Help me," she managed to croak out the words.

His brown eyes, buried beneath shaggy eyebrows, and a forehead creased with deep lines, softened. "Okay," he said, gently prying her hands from his shirt. "I'll help you, love, but first tell me your name. I'm Wade. Wade Crillick."

A calmness in the way he spoke soothed Paige's screaming nerves. His eyes were kind but lit with a wary intelligence that made her want to fall at his feet. Could it be possible that the nightmare was over and this man, who appeared out of the blue was here to save them?

"My name," Paige stuttered and for a split second her mind went blank. "My name's Paige Loche and ... And my husband is Hal."

He nodded down at her. "Okay, that's good. Now, Paige, tell me what happened."

"My husband." She gestured to the house. "He's badly hurt and Lizzy ... She's insane. She ..." Paige hesitated and glanced over her shoulder. Lizzy stood silently at the corner of the house, her face draped in shadows. "She cut off his leg so we couldn't leave." The tears poured down her face and her stomach heaved up and down.

Wade shook his head, a gesture of confusion, not disbelief. "Where's your husband now?"

"She's got him upstairs." Paige wanted to blurt out that Lizzy was after her baby, but her gut told her to just concentrate on the facts. "Please, we need help." She looked around for a vehicle and her eyes fell on the motorbike. Her stomach dropped. No way were they all leaving on the Harley. But then another idea occurred to her.

"You need to go and get help." She put her hand on Wade's arm and tried to turn him towards the bike. "You can bring back an ambulance and the police."

"Wait," he said pulling his arm away. "Just calm down and let me think."

"There's no time. You don't know what she's capable of. You need to go now!" Paige could feel herself shake with desperation.

Wade ran one weathered hand through his long grey hair. He seemed to be in the grips of a dilemma. "I can't just leave you here," he said. "If you think you're in danger, you should come with me." He nodded. "Yeah I think you should come with me and we can sort it all out when the cops get here."

"Listen," Paige said dropping her voice. "I can't leave my husband with her. She'll do something terrible." The last word came out in a wavering breath.

"Okay," he said and walked over to the bike. His boots crunched on the loose gravel. He threw his leg over with the practiced ease of a veteran biker. "I'm not sure what's going on here, but I'm calling the cops. I'll be a quick as I can."

Paige felt a sliver of heat in her chest, *hope*. She moved over to the bike where he sat with his forearms on the handlebars. She covered his deeply tanned hand with hers. "Thank you. I know it's a long drive, but …"

Wade frowned, his brows drawing together. "It's not that f-"

A thunderclap exploded in Paige's ears as something wet hit her in the face. Instinctively she ducked and wrapped her arms around her belly squeezing her eyes shut. The ringing in her ears made her shake her head from side to side. She let go of her stomach and covered her ears, but the sound seemed to be inside her head.

She opened her eyes. Wade had disappeared from the bike. She looked around expecting to see him standing next to her. She saw Lizzy holding a shotgun, its end looking like two black tunnels. The barrel of the gun slid down until it pointed at the ground.

Paige's throat worked and her mouth opened and closed, but she couldn't hear anything save the echo of the gunshot. Then a sudden swooping sound battered her ears as if a bird had flown past her.

Paige raced around the motorbike. Her worst fears were confirmed. Wade lay on his back, his long legs trailing out towards the bike. His arms were spread wide as if beckoning someone into a horizontal hug. Paige let out a whimper and folded down to her knees. His eyes were open and blinking rapidly up at the cloudless sky. His chest was a shredded mess of bone and tissue, blood oozed out of his mouth like thick dark oil.

"Wade," Paige said and touched his face with her trembling hand. "Oh God, I'm so sorry," she moaned.

He coughed and something dark and globular flew out of his mouth, landed on his chin, then slid down his neck. His moustache had turned from grey to red. He rolled his eyes towards Paige and blinked. A look of fear and pleading filled the previously warm orbs. A look that begged for help, but all she could do was sob powerlessly. A shudder began in his legs and then travelled up his body. He blinked once more then stilled. Paige had seen that look before. She knew he was gone.

"No. Wade! Wade!" She put her hand to his face. It was still warm but the skin as unresponsive as clay.

Paige slumped to the side and stared at her hands. They were smeared with blood. Wade's blood. She'd known him for less than five minutes and now he was dead. The breeze ruffled his hair and the smell of coppery, fresh blood and something else, something she didn't even want to acknowledge, filled her nose. Her stomach contracted and she dry heaved. Anything left in her stomach had come up at the dam.

She heard movement behind her and turned her head. "That was your fault," Lizzy said, her smoke-coloured eyes on Wade. "I just wanted him to go, but you couldn't let him. You had to drag him into this." She snapped her gaze away from Wade onto Paige. "Why did you make me do that?" She screamed and spit flew from her mouth.

She's losing it, the voice from the dark calculating place whispered in Paige's ear. *This wasn't part of her plan. She's not as crafty as she thinks.* Paige looked at the gun, if she could take it from her, she didn't doubt for a minute that she'd be capable of shooting the woman. She only needed one chance, a split second. The speed at which she'd turned her mind from Wade and back onto her own survival shocked her. She pushed the thought away.

Lizzy took a backward step and bumped into the bike. For a second Paige thought she would fall, but then regained her balance. Lizzy's face had drained of colour and her eyes moved between Paige and Wade's body. The woman was clearly crazy, but she genuinely seemed shocked by what she'd done.

Paige climbed to her feet, keeping her eyes on the gun. She wiped her forearm across her face, it came away bloody. She looked down and let out a gasp. Her dress was splattered with streaks of crimson. The intensity of the midday sun gave the blood a washed-out quality.

Lizzy, still holding the gun pointed down, turned away from Wade and walked towards the side of the house. Paige watched the woman's back, a patch of dampness darkened the fabric between her shoulders. A few flies clung to the circle of moisture. She was turning her back on the mess she'd created. Walking away as if she had something better to do. Paige could feel her blood pulse like fire and her hands curl into fists.

"What now?" She snapped and Lizzy stopped moving. "Someone will come looking for him." *Don't make this worse*, she warned herself but her mouth seemed to work independently. "You just killed a man and now you're walking away." Paige let out a harsh, humourless laugh.

Lizzy turned. Paige could see Soona near the corner of the house, hands flapping and head bobbing. Lizzy took a step towards Paige and let the shotgun hang loosely from the crook of her left arm.

"You brought him into this," Lizzy said. The shock and confusion had gone out of her eyes. Something else loomed over the woman's face – like watching storm clouds gather in a grey winter sky.

Paige knew she should stop; she could feel the anger coming off the woman in waves. But her own outrage exploded, taking on a life of its own.

"I know what you're doing," Paige said. "I won't let you." Her voice grew louder and the words spilled out. "I'll stop you, you maniac."

Lizzy crossed the gap between them in two steps. Before Paige could move to protect herself, the back of Lizzy's hand slammed into Paige's face. The blow caused Paige's bare feet to slide on the loose gravel; she hit the ground, landing hard on her left shoulder and thigh.

Her face smacked against the ground and pain sliced across her cheek. In the midst of the agony and surprise, she had time to acknowledge the strength in Lizzy's blow. She curled herself around her belly waiting for the next hit.

Lizzy leaned over her, blocking out the sun. "You make me sick," Lizzy spat. "You and your pretty-boy don't deserve that baby. But you're right about one thing." Paige could feel her hot breath on her face. "They'll come looking for him, but by then there'll be nothing to find."

"Baby, baby, baby," came Soona's voice shrill and panicked at Lizzy's shoulder.

Lizzy stood and the sun shone on Paige's face once more. "I know. I know," Lizzy snapped at Soona.

Paige sat up, the pain in her thigh and shoulder felt minor compared to the burn of her cheek. She put her hand on her face and felt a wet gash.

"Soona, wheel the bike around to the shed," Lizzy ordered over her shoulder and stomped away.

Soona leaned over Paige and slid her hand under her elbow. Paige stood, groaning like a senior citizen after aerobics class. Her side ached, but apart from the cut on her face, remained unhurt. She turned and looked at Wade's body. A deep, empty sadness crashed over her – for Wade, for Hal, and for her baby. Tilting her head, she stared up at the sky.

"I don't know how much more I can take," she said to the soft blue expanse. Her gaze moved across to the house. In the third window from the right, she saw her husband's face staring down at her.

Chapter Thirteen

Paige burst through the empty kitchen. Ignoring the smell of boiled vegetables and mould, she hurried into the sitting room. Her bare feet slapped the bland, threadbare carpet.

Hal was up, and out of bed.

She didn't know how he'd managed it, but she wasn't surprised. After everything he'd been through, most people would be ready to give up; but Hal wasn't most people.

She had only one thought, getting to him before Lizzy found him out of bed. In Lizzy's twisted mind, he was out of action and Paige wanted her to keep thinking that way. She paused in the hallway and listened. Silence, except for the occasional rattle of lose panes in the antique windows. Satisfied that Lizzy must be somewhere in her living quarters, Paige scurried up the stairs.

The door to Hal's room was closed, but not locked. Paige let out a relieved breath and pushed it open. Hal lay sprawled half-on, half-off the bed, his face the colour of wet newspaper and his chest heaving as though he'd just run a marathon.

"Paige, you're hurt," he managed through panting breaths.

After everything she'd seen today, the worry in his voice almost tipped her over the edge. It took tremendous effort not to cry.

"I'm okay," she managed to keep the tremor from her voice. "We've got to get you back in bed before she sees you."

She moved around trying to figure out the best way to get his trailing legs on the bed without hurting him.

He must have read her face. "There's no way to do it that won't hurt like hell. Just grab my broken leg and swing it up."

Paige took his ankle and hesitated. He braced himself on the sides of the bed and nodded. She lifted his leg and moved it onto the bed as he swivelled his hips. She could see him grimacing and closing his eyes, but there was no time to hesitate. Neither of them said it, but they both knew if Lizzy thought he posed any risk, she'd do something to incapacitate him further. Paige placed his leg on the bed as gentle as possible under the circumstances.

"The left one isn't as bad," he said around ragged breaths.

Paige lifted his left leg just above the bandaged stump. It was the first time she'd touched his leg since Lizzy had mutilated him. Even through the pain, she knew he'd be watching her reaction. The image of the foot under the water with the ribbons of flesh jumped to mind. She forced all the grief and helplessness off her face and swung his leg onto the bed.

She looked up, meeting his eyes. They were red rimmed and watery. "I love you," she said softly, before picking up the mess of tape, bandages, and equipment that littered the floor.

Satisfied the room was back as it had been before, Paige used the corner of the sheet to wipe Hal's sweat drenched face. She lifted the glass for him to drink. While he gulped down the water, she ran her hand over his damp hair.

"I know why she's keeping us here," Paige said. "The baby."

Paige's mouth dropped open. "How did you find out?"

Hal shrugged. "She's been rambling on about unwed mothers and girls in a jam all morning. It didn't take me long to work out she's fixated on the baby." He took Paige's hand and pressed it to his lips. "I saw what happened outside. If there ever *was* any way of talking her out of going through her insane plan, it's gone. Things have gone too far now."

Paige nodded. Lizzy had killed a man and once his wife, or whoever, reported him missing, it wouldn't be difficult to work out where he was. If Wade had family living with him someone might start looking as soon as tomorrow. If he lived alone it might take as long as a week. Either way, their stay at Mable House was nearing an end.

"I found our car," Paige said. "The keys are gone, but I'm going to look for them today."

Paige told him how Soona led her to the spot where Lizzy had hidden it. She'd decided she wouldn't tell him about the marron cages. If, when all this was over, it came out, there would be nothing she could do; but she wouldn't be the one to tell him. Not ever. He'd lost enough.

"Don't spend too long looking. If you can't find them quickly, just go and this time don't come back." He stopped speaking and put his hand to her face. "What she's done to you, I couldn't ..." His voice broke and he looked down.

"It's okay," she said quickly. "I can barely feel it."

* * *

Lizzy's voice rang out from the front of the house. Paige bolted across the room. Below, Lizzy and Soona stood over Wade's body. Lizzy pointed at Wade's shoulders and gestured for Soona to pick him up. Lizzy's thick hands curled into claws as she motioned up and down. It occurred to Paige that Lizzy looked like a witch

110

she'd once seen in a fairy-tale book she read to her year two class – large boned, scraggly hair, and menacing stance. Paige grimaced and turned away.

"They're outside moving the body. If they're planning on burying him, that'll give me at least an hour." Her indifference to the disposal of Wade's body startled her but it was something she'd have to deal with later.

"I'm going to search their rooms."

She headed for the door. On her way past, she stopped and kissed Hal. It was a soft lingering kiss on the mouth. She hoped it wouldn't be their last.

"Wait," Hal called. Paige turned at the doorway, her white dress looked like a butcher's apron. "When you find the keys, go. She won't wait for the baby to come. She'll take what she wants."

"I know," Paige whispered and closed the door behind her.

He was asking her to choose the baby and leave him to Lizzy's mercies. A choice which would condemn him to further torture and most probably death. *Once I'm gone why wouldn't she kill him?* Could she take that chance? With a two-hour drive to the roadhouse to summon help, how long would it before Lizzy set to work on her husband again?

Paige padded down the stairs. She couldn't think that far ahead. She had to concentrate her energy on forcing her fatigued mind and body to keep moving and focus on the next step, finding the keys.

She entered the sitting room, the long dusty curtains open half a metre or so allowed soft afternoon light to filter in, giving the already dated room a pearly glow. Tall shapes covered in dusty grey sheets occupied the centre of the room, leaving the corners empty, but for shadows and cobwebs.

Lizzy and Soona slept behind the sitting room in what Paige guessed must have originally been the caretaker's or housekeeper's quarters – if old hospitals had such things.

111

The area was directly behind the kitchen. She'd never been through the door at the far end of the disused room, and had no idea what to expect.

The solid wood door stood shrouded in shadows, peeling cream paint revealed a dark brown underneath. The knob, a circular brass grip, was battered with tiny dents. Lizzy and Soona passed in and out numerous times each day, so Paige had no reason to worry about it being locked. She put her hand out and grasped the knob, it felt sticky – probably the strawberry jam Soona lathered on her bread. The knob turned easily and the old door opened without so much as a creak.

Paige entered the dim room and closed the door behind her. The smell of boiled food and mould lingered, but was fainter than in the kitchen. There was something else though, an odour that lurked beneath the other smells, something unpleasant and musky. It reminded her of Lizzy. Paige wrinkled her nose and looked around.

She'd pictured a small room with two narrow beds and a bathroom, but the area behind the kitchen evolved into more of a suite. The room she stood in served as a small lounge area with two bulky brown armchairs, a worn nylon rug, and a small television on a squat coffee table. A sewing basket sat on the rug next to one of the chairs. The furnishings were more modern than the rest of the house, but still twenty years out of date.

Paige avoided the window at the far end of the room which, judging by its position, looked out onto the backyard. She skirted past the coffee table where the television sat surrounded by a cluster of framed photos. The bathroom was on the right, near where she'd entered, and two doors stood on the left, one open. A single bed and bedside table were visible. Paige inched forward, the sound of Lizzy's voice echoing in the distance.

A step further into the windowless room revealed dishwater grey walls, a small desk that looked like it belonged in a Victorian classroom, and six battered tins lined up along the far edge of the desk. In each tin rested a handful of pencils; they'd been divided by colour. Scraps of card that looked as if they'd been torn from food packages or cereal boxes were set out in rows. Crude drawings of cows covered every surface. Some were pinned to the wall above the desk. Paige picked up a piece of card that had been torn from a tea box. On the blank side was a drawing of a brown cow with a carrot in its mouth.

"You're as trapped here as we are," she said and looked up, startled by how loud her voice sounded.

She dropped the drawing and backed out of the room. She wouldn't find what she needed in Soona's room. Before she entered the other door, she stole forward and risked a look out the window. Wade's bike was parked near the shed on the far left. She couldn't hear Lizzy but the dull thud of a spade striking dirt came from somewhere out of view. Paige pinched her bottom lip between her thumb and forefinger. She had no way of knowing if Lizzy was still out there or if she'd left Soona to finish digging.

Paige crept over to the door leading to the sitting room. She cocked her head and listed for the heavy thud of Lizzy's rubber-soled shoes. A faint scuffling sound came from somewhere inside the house. Paige drew in a breath and held it. She leaned her head closer to the door and the scuffling turned into a rattle and then a thwack as the screen door leading to the back veranda slammed. Paige slapped her hand over her mouth to muffle a shriek. She looked around the room, eyes wide with panic.

Heavy footfalls thundered across the kitchen. Her first thought was to hide in the bathroom, but that might be where Lizzy was headed. Running out of options, Paige bolted for Soona's room. She stayed on her toes trying to minimise the impact of her feet on the boards. When she reached the doorway, she pivoted to her right with her hand on the knob. Her left foot slid out from under her and for a split second, she fell forward only stopping herself by grabbing the door with her left hand.

She pulled the wooden slab towards her and slipped behind it, standing sideways between the door and the wall. Her heart thrashed like a wild animal in her chest. She plastered her hands over her mouth to cover the raspy sound of her breathing and waited.

Chapter Fourteen

Hal used his arms to pull himself into a slumped sitting position. The strength in his forearms and shoulders felt diminished, he had a grim suspicion that his body was weakening and would continue to do so if he didn't get out of the bed. *Easier said than done.* Yes, but his mind told him he couldn't afford to let himself flounder. His body had been through tremendous trauma and he'd lost a good deal of blood. No doubt it had sapped his strength, but lying in bed sweating and thinking about the pain only made him more debilitated.

He pushed his fists into the bed and strained until his arms trembled. Slowly, he managed to move himself up until he sat with his back pushed against the metal frame. It wasn't huge progress, but he felt a slim flicker of pleasure. A door slammed below and anxiety replaced the momentary feeling of victory.

He had no way of knowing who'd opened or closed the door. It could've been Paige going outside, but he doubted it. Her plan had been to search Lizzy's room for the keys. He *had* told her to go straight away if she found them. Maybe that's what happened. He wanted to believe his wife and baby were anywhere but here. But he knew

Paige too well. She was loyal and fiercely protective, something he loved about her.

He listened to the sounds the old house made. Sounds that after only four days, he'd become accustomed to: windowpanes rattled, water trickled through old pipes and beams, and boards settled. Hal tried to sift through all the mundane sounds to pinpoint movement. He thought he heard another door open, but couldn't be sure.

He wanted nothing more than to be downstairs helping Paige, but wheeling himself across the room and sitting up were his big achievements for the day. As if on cue, the throbbing in his stump amped up a notch and a cold sweat broke out on his neck. Not only was he no help to his heavily pregnant wife, but worse, he'd become a liability. If it weren't for him, he had no doubt Paige would've left by now. He knew it and so did Lizzy. That's why she kept him alive.

If he wasn't such a coward, when he made it to the window he would've kept on going. Taken a swan dive and landed next to the poor bastard Lizzy shot in the chest. Then there'd be nothing to keep Paige from running. Lizzy would have no hold over her. Except it would destroy Paige and then she'd be here all alone. Hal tipped his head back and stared at the ceiling with its swirling patterns of damp.

Tears welled in his eyes; he rubbed them away with his fists. His wife was downstairs trying to outwit a murderer and he was sitting in bed crying. Kind of funny if you had a really sick sense of humour.

He rolled his head to the side, not knowing felt nearly as torturous as the sparks of pain in his broken leg. Hal looked at the trolley and wished he could ride it down the stairs. It wasn't such a crazy idea. He *could* try to use it to get to the lift and then down to the bottom floor. *Then what? Run Lizzy over with a nurse's trolley?*

He scratched his head and tried to think of something else. He was off the pain medication, that's why it felt like his legs were filled with broken glass, shifting and moving under the skin. But it should also mean that he could think more clearly. So far he had nothing.

Then it came to him. Something so simple and so obvious, he couldn't believe he hadn't thought of it sooner. Well, he had sort of when the crazy bitch leaned over him. He'd thought about hitting her with the water jug. Then it had been a fleeting notion, something he hadn't really taken seriously. But now, killing Lizzy seemed like a very good idea.

Chapter Fifteen

Paige shrank back as far as the limited space behind the door would allow. Hands still clamped over her mouth, she tried to calm her breathing and listen. Heavy feet moved around the far end of the room. A door clicked closed and, once more, the room fell silent. Sure that Lizzy was in the bathroom, Paige waited. After a few minutes she heard the sound of flushing followed by groaning pipes and running water.

Paige squeezed her eyes shut and waited, praying Lizzy would go back outside. The bathroom door creaked open and heavy feet stomped not away but closer to Paige's hiding place. In her mind, Paige pictured Lizzy flinging open the door and pointing the shotgun at her, its impossibly large barrels filling her vision and then, one last moment of horror before the woman pulled the trigger. It made perfect sense; Lizzy could blow her head off and still cut the baby out of her body before it was too late. *Maybe that's been her plan all along.*

The footfalls bypassed Soona's room and moved to the left. The doorknob clattered, and an errant floorboard squeaked. Lizzy was in her bedroom. Paige peeled her hands away from her face and pressed her ear to the wall between the two rooms. A chain of indiscernible noises followed, then what sounded like a drawer opening. Paige could faintly make out a tinkling, like a set of small bells.

Terrified that Lizzy would hear her breathing, Paige covered her mouth again. Lizzy's bedroom door closed with a snap and footsteps moved across the room. The tinkling turned into a jangling and Paige realised that the bells were in fact keys.

The steps halted, and Paige waited. For a moment nothing but the distant sound of birds twittering in the trees beyond the house filled the air. The moment seemed to expand and Paige wondered if Lizzy had left without her hearing. She began to lower her hands when she detected movement.

Footfalls scuffed back across the room, still heavy, but now slower. With each step came a metallic jangle. The sound suggested that Lizzy had put the keys in her pocket. As the jangling drew nearer, Paige became convinced that Lizzy had heard her or caught a glimpse of her through the door jam.

The air in the room felt heavy and stale. Tiny beads of sweat gathered on Paige's upper lip. The urge to wipe the moisture away became overwhelming, but she resisted for fear any movement, even the whisper of her skin against her dress, would be thunderously loud in the silence.

A board groaned outside Soona's room. In her mind's eye, Paige saw Lizzy standing in the doorway sniffing the air like a witch catching the scent of lost children. The image started a shiver at the base of Paige's spine, but she clenched her teeth and kept her body rigid. After a few seconds, Lizzy's footsteps moved away and withdrew. The door connecting the suite with the sitting room closed with a rattle.

Paige remained frozen behind the door, every nerve in her body hummed with concentration. It could be a trick – Lizzy pretending to leave then creeping back across the room so she could crouch on the other side of the door.

Paige made herself count to thirty, pausing between each number. When she'd finished, she hesitated, still unsure if it was safe to move. She thought of peeking around the door, but imagined Lizzy on the other side, bent over, large square teeth bared like a wolf.

Paige felt sweat run down her back. She remembered the way as a child the shadows had crowded into the corners of her own bedroom, like a witch uncurling out of the dark. Forcing the memory away, she looked around the room with wide eyes. *She* was a mother now; she had to be brave enough to stand up to monsters.

If she didn't move, she'd remain behind the door paralysed with fear until her legs gave out. She stepped out from her hiding spot and saw Lizzy on all fours grinning like a hyena. Paige gasped. The image changed into the shadow of the armchair.

She leaned back against the door jam and put her hands on her knees. She took two long, deep breaths, and then straightened up. She didn't know how long she had before Lizzy and Soona came back. She had to find the keys to the Ford, and quickly.

She opened the door to Lizzy's room. Weak light filtered through the flouncy curtains shielding the window. The first thing that struck her was the clutter. The room looked clean enough but photos filled the walls, embroidered cushions covered half the bed, and piles of letters and papers were strewn on the dresser and bedside table. A distinct odour assaulted her senses, sour milk mingled with that same musky scent present in the outer room.

Paige grimaced and pulled out dresser drawers filled with blouses, socks, nightdresses, and a selection of sensible – mostly beige – underwear. Next she searched the small drawers on the bedside stand. The top one contained the usual equipment: reading glasses, hand cream, toenail clippers. The second drawer was stuffed with old photographs. Paige lifted them and searched the bottom of the drawer. Nothing. As she placed the photos back, she noticed the one on the top was of Lizzy. A much younger, slimmer Lizzy.

Paige held up the photo, a colour snap taken at the front of the house. Lizzy looked about twenty, smiling happily in her nurse's uniform. Next to her stood a tall, hulking man in a grey suit, between them a dark-haired toddler staring vacantly to the side. There was something off about the scene but Paige couldn't quite put her finger on it. With no time to linger, she put the photo back and closed the drawer.

Next she tried the wardrobe. One thin black bar held a collection of old uniforms and a few skirts in brown and navy. *Nursing's not just her job, it's her whole life.* A tiny sliver of sadness scratched at Paige's heart. She pushed the thought away and reached up to search the top shelf. *If a person's hiding something, it's usually on the top shelf or in the bottom drawer.* She'd read that somewhere, most likely a mystery novel. It made sense though, the eyes first landed on what was in front of them, not above or below.

The top shelf sat a few centimetres above Paige's head. A brightly coloured vanity bag and a plastic tub filled the space. She could see the items on the edge of the shelf but not whatever lay hidden beyond them. She grabbed the bag and lifted it down, then turned and placed it on the bed. A circular zip secured the top of the bag. Paige unzipped it and opened the lid. The case was stuffed with blister strips of tablets, there had to be hundreds of them. Some were loose, others secured with elastic bands.

Paige read a few of the brand names, but the medications meant nothing to her. At least this solved the mystery of where she's been getting painkillers for Hal. Paige looked at a few more strips. Many of the names ended in *ine,* she was sure she'd read somewhere it meant the pills were morphine-based painkillers. She stuffed them back in place and zipped up the case.

Before returning to the wardrobe, she took a peek out the window. The flouncy curtains were covered in green and yellow daisies. An odd choice for a woman like Lizzy. There was a narrow gap where they'd been partially opened, about ten centimetres or so. Paige stood to the side of the gap and angled her head so she could see outside.

A narrow bar of the backyard showed. The doors to the large shed stood open. Paige could see Wade's bike parked nearby. Something metallic just beyond the doors caught a glimmer of sunlight. It was impossible to be sure, but she thought she'd caught a glimpse of a car farther back in the gloom of the shed. She stepped away from the window and inhaled sharply. How many vehicles were hidden on this property? And more frightening, where were their owners?

Paige stepped up to the window and ducked sideways when she saw movement. Sure that she was concealed by the side of the curtain, she risked another look. Lizzy ambled out of the shed. She emerged into the light like a bear coming out of a cave and tossed something aside. She wiped her arm across her face leaving behind streaks of dirt or oil.

Paige watched Lizzy regard the bike. Then the woman used her foot to hit the kickstand up and wheeled the black and silver Harley into the dark.

Satisfied that Lizzy was busy disposing of all traces of Wade, Paige returned to her search. She pulled the plastic tub down from the top shelf of the wardrobe. It was transparent, its contents – sewing paraphernalia – clear without the need to open it.

Paige dropped the tub and winced at the way it thudded on the scuffed boards. She hesitated before continuing her search. If Lizzy had heard, she'd be heading for the back door. After a minute or so she decided that the thud had probably been loud in the confines of the room, but not so loud as to carry outside.

She rose up onto her toes and tried to see the back of the shelf. There was something there, but the angle made it difficult to make out more than a dark shape. Stretching her arms as far as they would reach, Paige trailed her fingers along the back. Her hand touched something cold and solid. She pulled her fingers back as if stung, and then reached forward to hazard another touch. The object was cylindrical and smooth. She curled her fingers around it and slid it towards her. The barrel of the shotgun came into view.

"Yes." Paige muttered and pulled the gun down.

She laid it on the bed and reached up fanning her hand out and running it over the wood of the shelf. It closed over a box; she dragged it forward. A rolling came from inside. *Not many left, but it'll have to do.*

With the shells and the gun on the bed, she put everything else back on the shelf and closed the wardrobe. The beginnings of a plan formed in her mind. But something else gnawed at the edges of her thinking. Something important, just out of reach. She didn't have time to ponder, she had to find the keys.

The only place she hadn't checked was under the bed. Flipping back the chenille bedspread, she dropped to one knee. Her thigh and shoulder pulsed, a large plum-coloured bruise already spread across the top of her leg from where Lizzy's blow had sent her thumping to the ground. She bit her lip and crouched as low as her swollen belly would allow.

Two matching black cases were slotted next to each other, taking up almost three quarters of the space. *It's about time something went my way.* Paige pulled one of the cases out by the rim. A thin, yellow ribbon dotted with stars flopped around the handle. The ribbon had been Paige's idea. Before leaving for their honeymoon in Bali, she tied it on her case so she could tell hers from Hal's.

Paige grasped the ribbon between her fingers and rubbed it as if it had magical powers; that by touching it, she'd be transported back in time. The baby gave a sharp kick.

"I know, I've got to keep moving," she said and pushed the case back under the bed. It was Hal's case she needed.

She reached under and grabbed the corner. It was lighter than hers because he never seemed to need much when they travelled. Thankful for that, she pulled the case out from under the bed. It slid across the boards with a whisper. They hadn't bothered with locks this trip so opening it posed no problem.

How long has it been? It seemed like a few minutes, but it was probably closer to ten. She unzipped the case and flipped up the lid. Pushing back a pile of T-shirts, Paige and found what she was looking for.

For a second, she doubted what her eyes saw. After everything they'd been through, the sight of the spare car keys seemed too good to be true. Paige's hands shook as she snatched the keys out of the case and put them on the bed with the gun.

Shoving the case back under the bed, she used the side of her bare foot to sweep the dust balls that had been pushed free by the cases out of sight. She scanned the room, making sure nothing looked out of place. Her eyes came to rest on a stack of papers on the chest of draws. It looked like mostly old receipts, bills, and flyers. A letter folded in three segments, caught Paige's eye. It looked new compared with the rest of the pile. The bottom third of the page was unfolded and she could see the unmistakable stamp of a government department.

Don't, her mind screamed. *Get out now, before she comes back.* Her instincts told her to grab the gun and the keys and get moving, but something about that letter, the way it was perched on top of the pile, the unfolded end beckoned her closer like ghostly hand. Whatever secrets the letter held, wouldn't help her and Hal. The smart thing to do would be skedaddle. But instead of getting out of the room, Paige found herself in front of the dresser picking up the letter.

She unfolded the paper, her damp fingers almost sticking to the edges. It was from the Health Department and dated three months ago. Much of what was written was of no interest until Paige came to the second paragraph.

While we offer our condolences and gratitude in recognition of your father's many contributions to the health and wellbeing of our service men, without a licensed Medical Practitioner, Mable House Aged Care Facility is no longer eligible to serve as a licensed care facility. Under the Aged Care Act of 1974, in the absence of a General Practitioner, State and Federal funding shall cease and the facility will be required to suspend operation.

A Health Department representative will visit Mable House on the 29th of August to assist you in making arrangements for your remaining two residents to be transferred to Steven Tate Hospital in Albany.

Paige stopped reading. A few days before Lizzy stumbled upon Paige and Hal, Mable House had been closed *and,* judging by the tone of the letter, against Lizzy's wishes. Coming on top of the death of Lizzy's father, it could explain why the woman snapped. Paige had a feeling that Lizzy had always skated close to madness, but maybe her father and her work kept her from reaching the edge and diving into lunacy.

She folded up the letter and put it back on the pile. Knowing what set Lizzy on her path of kidnapping and murder wouldn't help Paige escape; if anything it only made the situation more terrifying because, with her father gone and the hospital closed, Lizzy had nothing to lose.

It was as if the temperature of the air changed. The hairs on Paige's arms stood up and she felt something sinister closing in on her; the feeling almost palpable in its intensity. Something was loose in the house. Something wild and ominous had broken free of whatever it is that keeps people from doing all the wicked things that whisper to them in their darkest moments. She could feel that something gathering force. She knew if she didn't get away from Mable House, it would infect her too.

Paige picked up the shotgun, noticing its weight, she hefted it under her arm then snatched up the keys and shells. She left the suite of rooms as quickly as possible, pausing only to close the door to the sitting room behind her. The back stairs groaned and the screen door clanked.

Paige froze, her legs felt heavy, as if filled with sand. The ancient floorboards in the kitchen groaned. Even if she knew how to load the shells into the shotgun, she'd never manage it before Lizzy reached the sitting room. She scanned the room looking for somewhere to stow the items. Running out of time, she flipped back one of the drop sheets covering the furniture. A cloud of dust flew up and swirled around her like mosquitoes. Underneath was a high-backed padded hospital chair. Holding her breath to avoid inhaling the dust, she put the gun, shells and keys on the chair and pulled the sheet over it.

Her impulse was to run upstairs and tell Hal what she'd found. She wanted to be anywhere but near Lizzy who, Paige feared, would know what she'd done just by looking at her. Instead of running, she pushed her shoulders back and walked into the kitchen.

It was as if nothing had happened. As though Lizzy hadn't murdered a man in front of Paige and then hit her to the ground. Lizzy, standing by the sink washing her hands, turned when Paige entered the room and gestured to a large metal pail sitting on the draining board.

"Fresh marron," Lizzy said pleasantly, her face still smudged with grease. "They're a good size too. I'm going to cook them as soon as I get some water boiling."

It took Paige a second to process Lizzy's words. It seemed Wade was forgotten and now it was time for this fresh horror. Paige could hear the crayfish scrambling over each other, their pincers clacking and hitting the inside of the pail. It sounded like bones scraping across a tin roof.

"I'm allergic to shellfish," Paige said, swallowing the sick feeling that threatened to turn into another bout of vomiting." She took a step forward and grasped the edge of the table as a wave of wooziness swept over her.

"You didn't mention that earlier," Lizzy snapped and tapped the side of the pail. The marron clattered frantically, a black claw appeared over the top.

"Didn't I?" Paige gave a dry chuckle. "I'm all over the place lately."

Lizzy held her gaze a little longer than necessary before turning away. "You'll have to fix yourself something then. I'm not cooking two meals; this isn't a hotel." She spoke rapidly, her words like machine gun fire.

The swing in the woman's moods, from pleasant to angry, was becoming worse. Or maybe Paige was more aware of the constant shift because she'd seen what Lizzy could do when she got angry.

"I'll just fix a sandwich for me and Hal, if that's alright?" Paige wasn't hungry, but she needed to eat. She needed her strength for the baby and to go through with what she had planned.

"Suit yourself," Lizzy said with a shrug, and started opening cupboards.

Paige pushed away from the table and made her way to the fridge on legs that felt like they were made of pudding. Her body was coming down hard from the adrenalin surge that started when Wade arrived and had carried her through the search of Lizzy's bedroom. Now she needed food and rest.

She opened the fridge and took out a block of cheese and a tomato. Then turned back to the table and opened the bread bin. She assembled the sandwiches in silence, sharing the room with the woman who had mutilated her husband and killed a man in front of her, as if all that had happened took a back seat to the mundane task of food preparation.

Lizzy lit the burner on the stove and a faint smell of gas filled the room. The woman turned from the stove and regarded Paige as if seeing her for the first time that day.

"Urgh, you're filthy," Lizzy said drawing her brows together. "I'll fetch you something clean to put on, but that dress will have to go."

I'm drenched in a dead man's blood. "Thanks," she said and sliced a cheese and tomato sandwich in half.

Lizzy bustled out of the kitchen. The door to her living quarters opened with a clack. *Did I close the bedroom door?* Paige stopped what she was doing and turned to listen. Had she left everything as she'd found it or was there something she'd overlooked? Paige tried to remember how far open Soona's door had been when she'd hid behind it. Would Lizzy notice if it had moved?

* * *

Paige found it difficult to breathe, her throat felt tight and constricted. She tried to cut another sandwich, but her hands shook too badly. She took a plate from the shelf over the stove, the crockery clattered in her grasp. The plate slipped from her hand, only saved by her quick reflexes.

When Lizzy came back into the kitchen, Paige didn't look up, afraid the anxiety she felt might be written on her face.

"Here," Lizzy said.

The crack of the woman's voice made Paige flinch. If Lizzy noticed anything amiss, she gave no indication. She tossed a grey dress over the top of one of the kitchen chairs.

"Put that on before you eat," she ordered. "Then give me that dress and I'll burn it. It's not the sort of thing a woman in your condition should be wearing in the first place."

She made it sound like disposing of evidence was the most natural thing in the world, and she was in fact doing Paige a favour by helping her correct a fashion blunder.

Paige wanted to scream in the woman's face, rage at her for what she'd done to Hal and Wade. The urge swept through her like a cyclone. She longed to open her mouth and let every ugly thought she had spew out. Maybe it was the constant fear or the shock of the things she'd seen or just the bombastic tone in Lizzy's voice when she ordered Paige to get changed, but Paige could feel herself tipping over the edge of sanity. It was like standing at the top of a steep flight of stairs and leaning forward. If you let yourself go, you'd be badly hurt, but pulling back keeps getting harder.

Paige looked down at the knife sitting next to the pate of sandwiches. It was no bigger than a steak knife with a dark brown handle held in place by a brass screw. If she picked it up and pushed it into Lizzy's thick, veiny neck, all her problems would be over.

Lizzy turned to the pail, reached into the bucket and pulled out a struggling marron. Without hesitation, she plunged the creature into the now boiling pot of water. It flayed and struggled, trying in vain to leap out of the scorching water.

Paige curled her fingers around the handle of the knife. *Would the woman's skin offer much resistance? How long did it take a person to bleed to death?* In the movies, it usually happened within seconds, but reality was much more brutal. Would Lizzy writhe on the floor for half an hour? *Good, do it*, the cold dark voice insider her urged. *Four days, that's how long it takes to torture someone into killing for survival*, Paige thought without emotion.

She held the knife at her side and stepped around the table. Across the room, she could see the back of Lizzy's neck, sun damaged and criss-crossed with lines. *Once you start stabbing, keep going till she goes down*, the voice whispered.

Three steps and she'd be across the room, directly behind the woman. She couldn't hesitate, she'd have to act before Lizzy turned. If she didn't strike immediately, and Lizzy realised her goal, she wouldn't get another chance. *She'll cut the baby out of your womb and let you die*, the voice warned. Paige knew it was true, time was running out. She had a plan, but this would be easier, quicker.

She took a step but the whack of the screen door halted her progress. Paige's head snapped around at the same time Lizzy's did. Soona shuffled into the kitchen, her jeans and shirt streaked with dirt, hands stained with grime. She stopped near the end of the table as if listening to a faraway sound that only she could hear.

Paige held the knife against her leg and stepped back to the sandwiches. Soona's distant countenance sparked a flicker of recognition that triggered a memory. She recognised her as the toddler in the old photo. Until that moment, Paige had assumed Soona was Lizzy's sister. They looked similar and Soona's age could be anywhere between thirty-five and fifty; it was difficult to tell. But now it dawned on her, *Soona is Lizzy's child.*

Paige snatched up the grey dress Lizzy had left for her and hurried through the sitting room. She'd been about to kill a woman in front of her own child. It hadn't been a passing thought; she'd really meant to do it. The detached coldness of her mind only a moment ago seemed ghastly. How could she have contemplated such a thing only hours after watching the life disappear from Wade's eyes? Paige looked down at herself, still covered in blood. It stained her dress, her face, even her legs.

She made it to the dormitory and closed the door. She leaned against the bed and sucked in huge breaths; shuddering sobs built in her throat. Paige stumbled into the tiny washroom and looked at her reflection in the mirror. Her hair stood up in wild peaks, flecked with red. A gash on her right cheek looked stark against her puffy swollen face. But most shocking was the look in her sunken eyes: haunted, vacant. Eyes so empty anything could take up residence behind them.

Paige realised she still held the knife. She tossed it in the sink; it struck the porcelain with a clank. She reached down and ripped the bloody dress over her head. It reminded her of the smell in the room after Lizzy cut off Hal's leg. She gagged and threw the dress on the floor. It landed on the cracked tiles with a wet plopping sound. She removed her phone from its hiding place in her bra, and put it near the dress.

Stripped down to her underwear, she turned on the cold tap, scooped up handfuls of water and threw them in her face, gasping at the cold shock. Desperate to cleanse herself, she grabbed the towel from the rack and soaked the end under the water. She used it to scrub her face and arms, then her chest. The air in the tiny bathroom grew heavy with the coppery smell of blood.

She ran the towel under the water again and again, scrubbing until her skin felt bruised and the cut on her cheek opened up. When she stopped, she was dripping wet, shivering in a puddle of water. Before turning away, she regarded herself in the mirror once more. *I'm slipping away. Lizzy's destroying me and something awful is trying to take my place.*

Paige pulled on the grey dress and felt the stiff fabric clinging to her damp body. It was too large, but it covered her from calf to elbow and helped ease the chills. She longed to curl up on the squeaky single bed and sleep. It would be such a release to close her eyes and forget, just for a while. The temptation to give up pushed against her will, but if she gave in, what would happen to Hal? The baby?

She stooped down and retrieved the phone; the battery was getting low so she turned it off. She'd need it later. For a moment she considered the knife, still sitting in the sink, a glimmer of light winking off the blade. She'd almost done something horrific. Something that would change her

131

in a way beyond recovery. She ran her finger over her bottom lip, then sighed and took it out of the sink. *Only if there's no other way*, she thought and shoved it in the deep pockets of her new dress.

Chapter Sixteen

Shadows crept across the floor in a pattern Hal had grown all too familiar with. Judging by the soft quality of the light from the small window and the elongation of the rectangle it cast on the scuffed boards, he guessed it must be nearly three o'clock. Not that time mattered much at Mable House. His days were an endless marathon of pain and fear. The only bright spot was Paige. In the moments they were together, he felt hope. And now that he'd made the decision to take action, his mind seemed clearer than it had since pulling into the carpark at the cheese factory.

But clear thinking wasn't enough, he needed to come up with a way to put thoughts into action. He surveyed the room: four walls, a cupboard, his bed and locker, a chair and the trolley. Not much to work with. He shifted his weight from one cheek to the other, his backside numb from sitting in one position. But nothing compared to the pain in his legs.

He forced his mind away from all that and back to the matter at hand. It had been more than an hour since Paige left in search of the keys. He had no way of knowing if she'd found them or if Lizzy caught her searching. Hell, Paige might have the keys and be driving off the property right now. No, if she was gone, Lizzy would've come straight up to his room and by now, another part of his body would be on hospital floor.

As much as he wanted to believe his wife and baby were safe, he knew sitting in bed with his ass going numb meant Paige was still here.

"Fuck," he swore aloud, just to hear himself speak.

Lying in bed, a helpless invalid, made him think of his father. A once strong, independent man, now frail and confused. At sixty-six, George Loche should have been enjoying his retirement. Playing golf, maybe even starting a romance with the woman that ran the local deli. Hal tried to remember her name - Lorna? Linda? Something with *L*. She had a thing for his old man, no doubt about it.

Hal recalled stopping at the shop with his dad, two or three years ago. The woman, Lisa. Yes, he was sure her name was Lisa, had red hair and a curvy figure. When his old man entered the shop, Lisa lit up. Her cheeks flushed with pleasure and there was a girlish quality to the way she said his dad's name. *George*, she made the word sound warm and pleasing on her tongue.

"She's got the hots for you," he'd told his dad on their way home.

"Cut it out." His father's face coloured, but there was a twinkle of devilish laughter in his voice.

Now his father wasted away in a home. His eyes ringed with milky confusion, sometimes crying when Hal visited him; he couldn't remember his son's name. Hal wondered if anyone bothered to tell Lisa why his father stopped dropping in for his daily paper. Maybe she noticed the old man going downhill and put two and two together? Still, he should've made the time to let Lisa know what happened.

Hal blinked away tears. *Fuck, I'm turning into a cry-baby.* He looked at the trolley next to his bed. An array of tape, gauze, and bandages, but nothing useful unless he planned on wrapping tape around Lizzy's mouth and nose to smother her. Watching her, the terror growing in her eyes as she struggled to breathe, would be satisfying but unpractical. His gaze drifted downwards and he frowned. Something slim and metallic stuck out from under the bed.

He craned his neck to the side and a pair of scissors with unusually long, pointed blades lay amongst the layers of dust covering the floor.

The clanging and gurgling of water echoed in the ancient plumbing system. Apart from a few doors closing, it was the first sign of movement downstairs in a long while. It could mean Lizzy was on the move. She might be getting ready to mutilate him once more. Just the thought gave him the jolt he needed to get moving. He gripped the left side of the bed, along the metal bar below the mattress, and gradually leaned his body over the right side, his arm outstretched.

The movement lifted his left hip off the bed and with it his thigh. His stump shifted to the left and barbs of pain swirled in his severed bone. He hissed through his teeth, froze like a tightrope walker trying to regain his balance. He allowed himself a couple of shaky breaths, then continued reaching under the bed.

His fingers brushed the floor. He could feel a fine film of dust moving under his touch. He turned his head to track his progress. The handle of the scissors was less than five centimetres away. He swallowed hard then leaned out farther. This time his stump protested, but with less force than he expected. His forefinger curled around the handle and he looped the scissors onto the crook of his finger.

"Yes!" The cry of triumph came out as a croak. Then, "Oh shit." As his left hand slipped. He almost lost his grip on the bed.

Dropping the scissors, he watched in dumb silence as they skittered under the trolley. He stared at them as he leaned over the edge of the bed, his mouth hanging open in disbelief. He had them. The handle had looped around his finger. All he needed to do was straighten up and he'd managed to fuck it up. *How are you going to kill that crazy woman if you can't even hang on to a pair of scissors?*

"I'm not done yet," he said to himself and grabbed the leg of the trolley.

If he rolled it back towards the bed, he might be able to push the scissors closer. It was worth a try. All he had to risk was falling out of bed, landing on his broken leg, and squirming on the floor in agony. He gave a humourless chuckle and pulled the trolley towards him.

The back wheel snagged the circular handle of the scissors and pushed it in the direction of the bed. Hal resisted the urge to cheer, and kept the trolley steady on its course. Sweat ran down his nose and landed in small plops on the floor.

Hal let go of the trolley and gripped the long blades of the scissors. This time, he carefully clenched his hand around them before trying to lift himself back into bed. The boards on the landing outside his room groaned. He had less than two seconds to hoist himself into a sitting position and get the scissors out of sight.

His left arm quivered but held. He worked every ounce of strength he had in his bicep and pulled himself into a sitting position. In one fluid motion, he swept the scissors under his pillow. As his hand disappeared behind him, the door rattled and opened.

"Paige." It came out as a deep exhale.

Hal sagged onto the bed and blew out another breath. A jagged pain pierced his chest and he wondered if thirty-two was too young to have a heart attack.

"Hal," she said, her eyes wide with concern. "Are you in pain? You're covered in sweat."

She held a plate of sandwiches in one hand, and closed the door behind her with the other.

"No. I'm fine. I've just been leaning over to pick something up," he said and pulled the scissors out for her to see. The light glinted off the blades giving them an evil gleam.

Paige grimaced and put the sandwiches on the locker. She looked different; sure, she'd changed her clothes, but different in a way he couldn't quite put his finger on. She leaned over him and pressed her lips against his. They felt soft and cool, but the kiss was tight. He circled her in his arms and traced his hands over her back. Her shoulders felt small and frail, the bones more pronounced then he remembered.

"I found the keys," she whispered.

When she pulled away, he noticed the dark smudges under her eyes and the thin line now etched between then. She looked exhausted and fragile. All his struggles and worries seemed petty and selfish. She'd witnessed a murder, been hit to the ground, and then searched the house while a mad woman hovered nearby. She'd done all this only months from giving birth.

"Paige, I want you to stay here with me. When Lizzy comes in, I'm going to kill her. That's why I've got the scissors."

She shook her head and sat in the chair facing him. "I can't stay. Too many things could go wrong." Her mouth was set in a thin line and her blue eyes flittered around the room. She looked skittish, as if having trouble staying seated.

"I can't keep letting you go out there and risk yourself and the baby," he said gently.

"You're the one who told me to go and not come back," Paige snapped.

The edge in her voice surprised him. It must've shown on his face because the next time she spoke her tone was more controlled. "Just hear me out. I've given this a lot of thought and I think it'll work."

"I can't protect you out there," he gestured at the door. The more he thought about it, the more he was determined she stay.

"You can't protect me in here," she said in a flat emotionless voice he barely recognised.

137

The impact of her words made Hal flinch inwardly. *She's saddled with a cripple*, Lizzy's voice echoed in his mind. He'd tried to believe he was still the same man, but even his own wife didn't trust him to protect her. Not when it came down to life or death. He was a liability to her *and* the baby.

"I'm sorry if that sounded harsh," she said softly. "But I won't hide in here and wait for her to come and get me."

Hal nodded and glanced at the scissors in his hand. They looked small. He didn't blame Paige for not trusting his ability to keep her safe; when push came to shove, he couldn't even stand.

She put her hand over his. "Just hear me out. I think there's a way to get us both out of here without the need for any more bloodshed."

He wanted to pull her into his arms and promise her he could protect her. But he knew the man he'd been four days ago was gone. Lizzy's words rang in his ears, shaking him in their grip. The best thing he could do for his wife was to let her go. He nodded for her to continue.

"When I was searching for the keys, I found the shotgun. When she's asleep, I'll bring it in here and leave it with you. That way, if she comes up here and tries anything, you can protect yourself and …"

"Wait." Hal held up his hand. "If you have the shotgun, just give it to me now and we'll wait for her. Or call her in here." He paused. "I know I'm not … Not what I used to be, but I can still fire a gun."

"Hal," she said. "You haven't changed." But as she spoke, her eyes shifted to the window and her fingers twisted nervously in her lap. "It's not about how weak or strong you are; it's about getting us out of here in one piece. If you miss, she might have other guns." She circled her arm in the air. "Or, she might leave us here to starve. She's capable of anything. I won't take the chance." She looked back at him and held his gaze. "I won't let *you* take the chance. I can't lose you." The last four words came out clipped and wavering.

He wanted to argue, but knew she was right. If his aim was off, Lizzy could get away and come back shooting. They couldn't risk a gun battle, not with the baby to think about.

"Okay," he said. "Tell me the plan."

He listened to her talk with a growing mixture of excitement and unease. She started slowly and then her words tumbled out in an urgent whisper. He'd never seen his wife like this. A stranger, who looked like Paige, had taken her place. He'd always known she was strong, stronger than she gave herself credit for, but this woman was fearless and determined. The detached quality to her stare seemed alien on a woman who couldn't watch sad movies because they upset her for days.

When she'd finished, she said, "Well? What do you think?"

But Hal knew what she was really asking. "Yes, I'm up to it," he said, and hoped to God he was.

Chapter Seventeen

Paige left Hal's room and placed the empty plate on the floor. She walked past the stairs trying to make as little sound as possible, but the third-floor landing was a mine field of squeaky boards. The first room she tried was empty except for a stack of stained mattresses. The next, a small windowless room that smelt like disinfectant. Paige snapped on the light next to the door and a single bulb buzzed to life. The room looked like some sort of operating theatre with a set of deep metal sinks and trays of instruments on trolleys. The floor was covered in dark green vinyl with patches of brown in a few areas. Paige grimaced, turned off the lights, and shut the door.

The third door along the landing opened into another dormitory-style room. Two rectangular windows along the far wall were covered with rotting boards; thin streaks of grey light dropped through the gaps between the wood. The room looked similar to the one Paige slept in except here, the beds lay in pieces on the bare wooden floor, at the far end chairs and various hospital equipment were stacked in a haphazard pile. Paige tip-toed out of the room to the banister and looked down. The vacant lift, like a giant mechanical cave, took up much of the landing. By standing to the left, she could see all the way to the tiled entrance hall.

The ground floor was devoid of movement. From above, the swirling pattern made by the black and white tiles on the foyer floor looked like a large black snake. Satisfied that Lizzy wasn't around, Paige slipped back into the dormitory room and selected the piece of equipment she'd need for later that night. She left her find near the door and backed out of the room.

There wasn't much more she could do now but wait until nightfall. She picked up the plate she'd left near Hal's door and walked down the stairs.

In the kitchen, the lights filled the room with a stark yellow glow. Lizzy and Soona were seated at the table, their heads bent over deep bowls. When Paige entered, Lizzy looked up, a line of pearly soup dripped from the corner of her mouth. Paige thought of the bait the marron feasted on and resisted the urge to gag.

"Sit down will you?" Lizzy dabbed at her mouth with a cotton napkin.

"I'll just wash this," Paige gestured to the plate in her hands and headed for the sink.

"Leave it." There was no mistaking the order in Lizzy's voice so Paige set the plate down in the sink and took her place at the table. The thick, sweet smell of cooked crayfish hung in the air. She swallowed her disgust and sat next to Soona, who held a spoon in one hand and a chunk of bread in the other. She continued to slurp soup as Lizzy spoke.

"That dress is much more suitable."

Paige pulled on the stiff collar and nodded. She glanced at the clock on the shelf over the stove, only six-fifteen. It would be at least two hours before Lizzy and Soona went to bed.

"How are you feeling?"

The question took Paige by surprise. Her confusion must have been obvious because Lizzy repeated the question.

"How are you feeling?"

"I … I'm alright," Paige managed, unsure what to say. *I'm sick to my stomach with fear and revulsion. I've been terrorized and hit and my husband's been mutilated, so just fine.*

"The baby moving much?" Lizzy asked over a spoonful of chunky grey liquid.

So now we get to it, Paige thought. *The reason we're here. The real reason.* "Yes." She tried to give little away. Even talking to the woman about the baby made Paige jumpy.

"When I had Soona, I could tell something was wrong. I'd been around enough pregnant girls to know the baby's supposed to move." She shrugged. "Soona only gave the odd ripple, I was very young, but I knew it wasn't right." She stopped eating and looked over at Soona. "My father told me everything was fine, but I knew." Her mouth quivered, it was a tiny movement and then she let out a long, tired breath. "A mother knows; don't you think?"

"I think I'd know if something was wrong," Paige said, folding her arms around her bump. "But this is my first baby so …" her voice trailed off.

Lizzy nodded and took a spoonful of soup. She lifted it to her mouth then paused. "Do you know the sex?"

They'd made the decision not to find out the baby's gender. Paige remembered Hal said something about enjoying the surprise. He'd been so excited about being a father that she'd thought he'd insist on knowing if he was going to have a son or a daughter, but he was adamant that it was better to wait. She pictured Hal's green eyes twinkling over the top of his sunglasses as he pressed his hand to her belly, and her eyes blurred with tears.

"No, we don't know." She looked down at her arms lying protectively over her belly.

Lizzy nodded and shovelled the spoon into her mouth. "Lots of babies have been born here. I had Soona here.

Right upstairs." She used her spoon to point up at the ceiling and drops of soup ran down her wrist. "After she was born, my father sent me away to study nursing in Albany."

"That must have been hard for you," Paige said, trying to sound sympathetic.

Lizzy picked up a slice of bread and tore off a chunk. She dipped it in her soup and pushed it into her mouth without answering. Her teeth and lips worked like a mulching machine. For a few minutes the only sounds were the ticking of the clock and the clatter of Lizzy and Soona's spoons.

"He said it would be better for me not to get too attached. He was going to have Soona adopted, but once it became obvious she was retarded, no one wanted her." Lizzy gave a shrug and popped another chunk of bread in her mouth.

"What about your mother? What did she say?" Paige asked, genuinely interested. *Something* had happened in this isolated house that ultimately led to her and Hal's current predicament. Whatever secrets were hidden in Lizzy's past brought her to a place where the death of her father and the closing of Mable House pushed her over the edge. Those two events triggered whatever insane scenario Lizzy was intent on playing out. Suddenly it seemed important to know more.

Lizzy gave a snort, a sound somewhere between a laugh and a grunt. It reminded Paige of a pig. "She was dead by then. Not that she'd have been any help anyway." Lizzy pointed her spoon at Paige. She was like you; one of those pretty fragile types. Life out here got too much for her." Their eyes locked and Lizzy seemed to be studying her. "Although, I think there might be a bit more steel behind those baby blues than you let on." Lizzy licked her mouth, her tongue startlingly red against her pale lips.

All sorts of questions flooded Paige's mind. She wanted to ask about Soona's father, but she had a sick feeling in her stomach that Lizzy's relationship with her own father was pivotal to the situation.

Ignoring Lizzy's dig at her, Paige persisted. "Did your father send you away because you got pregnant?"

The silence stretched. Lizzy still held the spoon, she dipped it in the dregs of her soup and swirled it around. Paige wondered if she'd gone too far. Maybe asking about her relationship with her father would set off another angry attack. She steeled herself and moved her right hand from her belly and slipped it in her pocket. She felt the handle of the knife.

"He was under a lot of pressure," Lizzy said after a long silence. "He loved me. I helped him keep this place going." Her grey eyes looked watery as if she were fighting tears. "He needed me. It's not easy to be responsible for everyone … sometimes the stress got to be too much."

Paige wondered if Lizzy was still talking about herself or her father. She felt a tiny pang of pity for the woman, then just as quickly she pushed the feeling away.

Lizzy dropped her spoon into the bowl with a sharp clang. "What happened today with Wade, I didn't mean to do that," she said changing direction. "Wade was a good man, not like some of the ratbags in town."

"Did he have a family?" Paige asked hoping her question wouldn't provoke the woman. It was the longest conversation they'd had since Paige first flagged down Lizzy's ute. Part of her wanted to know more about the woman capable of inflicting so much pain, but another part wanted to shrink from Lizzy as if the madness that raged in the woman's mind could be contagious.

"There's time," Lizzy said. "His wife died four years ago and his son lives in Darwin." Her eyes were calculating and a smile played around the corner of her mouth. The tears glossing her eyes only seconds ago were gone so fast Paige wasn't sure if they'd ever been there.

"Time for a cuppa," Lizzy said jovially, and stood up.

Chapter Eighteen

Paige paced the room, her bare feet slapping on the scuffed boards. It was still too early to make a move. She'd left Lizzy and Soona in the kitchen almost an hour ago, but when she crept out to listen, the sound of the television floated from their living quarters. Paige stopped pacing and sat on the narrow bed.

The dormitory was lit by a single naked bulb hanging from a twist of wires. The light cast shadows in every corner giving the room an eerie feel. She patted her pocket and felt the outline of the knife. If everything went to plan, she wouldn't have to use it. She clenched one hand over the other and drew them up to her mouth. Her body fought heavy fatigue, and the muscles in her back felt bunched and tight. She'd only managed a few hours of sleep last night. In the last three nights, she'd slept very little, and during the times she had found deep sleep, she'd been plagued by nightmares.

She tucked her legs up onto the bed and leaned sideways until her head rested on her right arm. Sleep would be an escape, if only a short one. She longed for a few moments of black nothingness where she could hide from the ugly reality that shadowed each waking hour.

Paige locked her eyes on the door. The wood was painted a shade of green that was probable once minty and cheerful, but now faded to the colour of boiled cabbage.

She was probably safe for tonight, but if she didn't get away soon, Lizzy would come for her. Killing Wade had narrowed Lizzy's window of opportunity. The fact that Wade had no family to report him missing would give her a little wiggle room, but sooner or later the police would come calling. That meant within the coming week, Lizzy would take what she wanted and dispose of Paige and Hal.

Paige draped her arm over her belly and felt the gentle movements of her baby. She couldn't let that happen. The small innocent life inside her shifted, oblivious to the danger. Paige closed her eyes and hummed a lullaby she remembered from her own childhood. The baby settled and Paige let out a sigh. Her eyes fluttered open and checked the door one more time before she sank into sleep.

* * *

She was in her father's bedroom, the sheets were rumpled and washed in early morning light. She called out, but her dad didn't answer. Her heart pounded in her throat and her ears buzzed. She reached out and touched the chest of drawers near the wall and felt something land on her hand. She tried to flick it away thinking it was a fly — it's always a fly. But the thing on her hand hung on, too heavy to be an insect.

In her dream, Paige looked down at her hand and gasped. A thick, dark green snake curled around her wrist, its pink fleshy mouth gaping open to reveal a long blue tongue. She shrieked and shook her arm sending the snake flying across the room.

She headed for the bathroom calling out to her father as she stumbled through the door. Her father lay sprawled on the black tiles. His face turned to the floor and his arms stretched out in front of him as though he were getting ready to dive through the floor.

"Dad? Dad, are you alright?" Paige cried out, knowing he wasn't. He would never be alright again.

The buzzing in her ears grew louder, almost deafening. She sank to her knees when she noticed her father's legs, they were both nothing more than bloody stumps sticking out of his blue-striped boxer shorts. Ribbons of red and white flesh left a trail of blood smeared on the black tiles. It looked like he'd crawled across the floor.

Paige moaned and reached out to touch his shoulder, but flinched back when his head snapped up. She stumbled back, her mouth open but refusing to make sounds. It was her father's body, but Hal's tortured face stared up at her. When he opened his mouth a swarm of flies buzzed out. Paige's chest pumped up and down until finally, she pushed out a scream.

She scrambled on the floor next to the bathroom door trying to get to her feet, but her arms were caught by squirming snakes that held her down and slithered over her skin. She jerked back trying to free herself and her eyes sprang open. For a moment, the glare of the light baffled her, she felt something touch her cheek and shrieked.

* * *

Paige swatted at her face with her right hand before realising that she was hitting herself. She'd fallen asleep on her left arm and her numb fingers brushed against her cheek. Still breathing hard from the nightmare, Paige sat up and rubbed her left hand until painful pins and needles flooded her lifeless limb.

Her eyes darted to every shadowed corner, the light seemed shockingly bright over the bed, but in the corners anything could lurk. She had no idea how long she'd been asleep. The back of her dress felt damp with sweat. She swung her legs over the edge of the bed and waited for the sense of confusion to dissipate.

Over the last thirteen years, she'd had countless dreams about the morning she'd found her father dead on his bathroom floor, but this one was by far the worst. The terrifying images wouldn't leave her mind and her hands shook with fear. She closed her eyes and saw Hal pulling his severed legs across her father's bathroom. She forced the image away and sat on the edge of the bed breathing in and out slowly. There was too much at stake tonight to let a nightmare sap her strength.

After a few minutes, she felt calmer and her hands were steady. She pushed the stiff grey fabric of her dress aside and pulled the phone out of her bra. When Paige looked at the blank screen, despair flooded her until she remembered it wasn't flat, just turned off.

"Come on," she said. "Get your shit together."

I'm trying, she thought and turned the phone on. Eleven-twenty and less than a quarter charge left in the battery. *It'll have to do.* Paige left the phone on and shoved it back in her bra. She opened the dormitory door and let the light spill across the foyer. She crept across the entry, the tiles icy under her feet. When she reached the darkened sitting room, she paused and listened. Outside an owl hooted softly and the wind rustled trees and rattled the windows.

This moment had been building in her thoughts all afternoon. Part of her mind thumped with fear, dreading what was to come; yet another part of her no longer wanted to pass the buck and wait for someone else to save her skin. That piece of her was eager to get going.

A small whisper of doubt ran through her. *What if Lizzy knows what I'm up to and took the gun and the keys?* Paige moved around the bulky furniture and found what she was looking for. She flipped the dust sheet off the hospital chair and gave a small grateful sigh when the gun, shells, and keys were still on the oversized padded sofa.

She grabbed the car keys and put them in her pocket with the knife. She carried the shotgun and the box of shells and headed upstairs. The light from her room spilled out enough glow for her to see up to the second floor, but after that the darkness swamped her. She juggled the gun and the shells trying to get to her phone. Finally, she put the gun on the floor and pulled out her phone.

"Thank God for smartphones," Paige whispered and turned on its light.

She snatched a look over the banister, reassuring herself Lizzy wasn't lurking below, and picked up the gun. The double-barrelled pump-action shotgun had a thick stock made out of some sort of heavy wood. Awkward to carry, its bulk and weight were reassuring. She'd heard it go off and seen the carnage it could wreak, a grim but comforting thought.

The three-storey climb was difficult at nearly thirty weeks pregnant, but when you throw a shotgun into the mix, it becomes a slog. By the time she reached the third floor, her arm muscles shrieked with protest and her thighs burned with lactic acid. She stopped at the top of the last step and leaned against the banister. She didn't want Hal to see her struggling, he was already reluctant about the plan. If it looked like too much effort, he'd try and talk her out of going on.

Paige put the gun and the phone on the floor and stretched her arms over her head. She pistoned them in and out a few times then rolled her shoulders. Her legs still felt stiff; if she made it to tomorrow, she supposed she'd suffer for it. *If I make it to tomorrow, I'll be high kicking regardless of what shape my legs are in*. She picked up the shotgun and phone and took the last few steps to Hal's door.

The light from the phone cast a blue veil over the bed. Hal was sitting up, eyes wide and skin an eerie grey colour. The image of Hal on her father's bathroom floor flashed across her mind.

"I was starting to think something went wrong," he said.

Paige put the shotgun on the bed and grasped his face in her hands. His cheeks felt warm and the four-day growth of whiskers rasped against her palms. "I'm sorry you were worried," she whispered, trying to keep her voice steady. "Everything's fine."

She held his face for a second longer and looked into his green eyes, just to reassure herself he was real and the dream was gone. Hal was alive and safe, for the time being.

He held her wrist and slid her hand to his mouth. "I know you're set on doing this, so I won't try to talk you out of it." He kissed her palm and then pulled her against him so his cheek pressed against her belly. "All I care about is the two of you getting away from here."

"I know," Paige ran her fingers through his hair. She missed his touch. She wished this nightmare was over and she could climb into bed and curl herself around him.

"If there's any ..." he hesitated. "Any problems, just go." Paige started to protest, but he cut her off. "I can take care of myself. The last time – when she, you know – I was drugged to the eyeballs and not expecting it. She won't get another chance like that."

Paige pulled back. "I have to get going. The light on my phone won't last long." She dropped the box of shells on the bed. "Can you load this while I get everything ready?"

Paige turned and slipped out of the room. When she returned Hal held the shotgun, sliding the shells into the breach. He cocked it up and down. "There were only two shells in the box so if you have to use it, make them count." He handed her the gun.

"No. Keep it with you. If she comes through the door, shoot her." Paige pushed the gun back towards him.

Hal's face tightened. "I'm not going to argue with you about this," his words were harsh, she'd never heard him like this. "I'm not a defenceless cripple. Take the gun."

She wanted to protest, but knew it was useless. Time was short and she had to go. Besides, if they were going to get through this night, they'd have to have faith in each other.

"Okay. I love you," she whispered, and kissed him. "Give me about an hour before you move." She picked up the shotgun and turned to leave.

"I love you." Paige heard him answer as she closed the door and left him in the dark.

Chapter Nineteen

Paige leaned the shotgun against the side of the backstairs taking care to make as little sound as possible. Before leaving the house, she turned off the light in the dormitory and closed the door. If Lizzy woke, Paige hoped she'd assume everyone was asleep.

She lowered herself to the second step from the bottom and winced as her thighs protested and the stair creaked. The moon, partially hidden behind gauzy grey clouds, offered only the faintest silver light. Most of the yard remained in darkness, the sheds and grevillea bushes only recognisable as jagged black outlines. By the light of the phone, Paige slipped on her dirty tennis shoes. They were dry now, but the canvas felt stiff and unyielding against her feet.

She used the banister to haul herself up, and picked up the shotgun. She felt strangely light, as if the weight of her belly had lessened somehow. Not unpleasant, but unsettling in its newness. *Adrenalin*, she told herself and hoisted the gun into the crook of her arm.

The wind kicked up a notch and the associated rustling and rattling provided noise cover. Not that crossing the yard was noisy, far from it. Paige followed the small arc of blue light past the Hills Hoist and towards the bushes. Once she was on the other side of the grevilleas, she'd be out of sight.

She rounded the bushes and a scraping thump brought her to a halt. She sucked in air as if jolted by an electric shock and fumbled with the gun. The light bounced around and slid from her hand, hit the ground, and landed near her feet. Her head snapped left and right searching for the source of the faint sound. Without the light, it was impossible to see more than a metre in front of her.

Paige clenched the handle of the gun and lifted it higher, without the light she had no idea where to aim. Her head still moving back and forth, she crouched down and snatched the phone out of the grass. This time she nearly lost her grip on the gun. She tightened her grasp and stood up.

Blood rushed through her ears and her breath came in sharp barks. If Lizzy had been walking behind her, Paige probably wouldn't have heard her over the wind and her own panicked breathing. She moved the light in a wide arc, observing as much as possible before taking another step.

The noise had come from the left and at least a few metres ahead, somewhere in the direction of the sheds. *Could Lizzy be hiding in a shed?* It was possible. Maybe she'd heard Paige go upstairs and dashed outside to wait for her. Paige bit her bottom lip and stepped forward. She stretched out her arm trying to throw the blue beam as far as possible.

The coarse fabric of her dress blew against her legs as her hair flew forward over her face. She shook her head and turned back towards the house. It stood in darkness. Just on the other side of the bushes, she could distinguish the huge outline of the Edwardian building but with no interior lights.

Gun in her right hand, held just above her hip, and the phone in her left, Paige stepped forward. There came another noise. It sounded like fingernails scraping metal.

Paige froze. A cry of terror built in her throat, big and solid like an avocado pit. She clenched her mouth and raised the phone higher. The blue light trembled, landing on one of the sheds.

She resisted the urge to call out. In her mind she was already formulating what she'd say when Lizzy stepped out of the shadows. *I've got the gun. Stay away from me or I'll shoot you.* Even in her head, her voice sounded weak. Where was that cold dark voice that had whispered in her ear?

Paige let out a shuddering breath and edged closer to the shed. The light played over the grey wood of the walls. Bathed in the blue of her phone, the building looked washed out and grey like ancient bones. She skimmed the light over the grimy windows and up to the roof. When the glare hit the joint between wood and tin, another scraping shook the building. This time it sounded closer, frantic. The light made contact with something yellow and reflective. Paige sucked in air and then relaxed.

A creamy brown possum turned and pushed itself through a narrow gap under the roof. It disappeared inside, curly tail sliding after it. Paige realised her shoulders were hunched around her neck. She let them slump down and tipped her head back at the inky sky. *A bloody possum*, she almost laughed. *I nearly shot a possum.*

Before walking on, she skimmed the light around the building just to be sure nothing else lurked in the dark. Apart from a few spiders, the shed looked unoccupied. Paige stole another glance back, but the bushes obscured her view of the house. It was as though the yard had closed around her. The thought of walking across the huge property at night seemed like the easiest part of her plan, but now every nerve in her body jangled on edge. Every sound and every shadow seemed menacing and sinister. *I'm a city girl*, she thought and let out a dry laugh that sounded more like a moan when it hit the wind.

Only this morning, Soona had shown her the way to the car; with the sun shining, every detail of the property was crisp and clear. In the dark, the difficulty lay in remembering which way to turn. By the time Paige cleared the sheds, she could smell the rich aroma of freshly turned earth mixed with the sharp smell of tomato plants. *The earth hadn't been freshly turned this morning*. Paige remembered the tomato plants, but they'd been at least a metre and a half high. That meant that they'd been planted some time ago.

Worried that she'd taken a wrong turn, she played the light to her left across the rows of vegetables. The taller plants shimmered as the wind rustled through their dark leaves. She could make out smaller plants and seedlings by their outlines. Then an area about the size of a surfboard stood apart from the rest of the greenery. The earth had been piled over in a mound. Along the centre ran a neat row of seedlings, each plant about ten centimetres high. It looked and smelled fresh. Paige frowned and moved to continue when realisation hit her like a cold shower on a hot day – Wade.

She shivered, not from the wind, but with the realisation that if she didn't get them out tonight, there'd be two more new plots in the veg patch. It didn't matter that Lizzy couldn't possibly hope to get away with what she'd done *or* what she planned to do. Lizzy had made up her mind and nothing would shift her from the course she'd set for herself. If there'd been any doubt in Paige's mind that the woman would carry her plan through to the end, Wade's makeshift grave put it to rest. Paige turned away and plodded on towards the paddock.

The soggy grass underfoot told her she was getting closer. Grateful for the feeling of lightness the adrenaline had given her, she lifted her knees and took loping steps to avoid the marshy ground sucking her down. The smell of manure hung thick and heavy in this area, but it was not distasteful. Paige glanced over at the paddock, the cows were silent hulks against the dimness.

The barn rose like a tombstone out of the blackness, its peaked roof cutting a sharp outline against the cloudy expanse. The entrance to the trail was somewhere between the end of the paddock and barn. Paige readjusted the shotgun against her hip and felt the twinge of a cramp in her side. She'd been carrying the hefty gun for at least fifteen minutes, balancing it against her side and hip. She considered stopping and swapping hands, but the ground was too soft. If she stopped for any length of time, her feet would sink.

The feel of the dampness seeping into her shoes and squelching against her soles made her hurry. The stiff edges of her tennis shoes scraped against her ankles and the beginnings of cluster blisters carved their way into her skin. Her thighs trembled with the effort of lifting her legs so high. *A few more steps and I'll be clear of the mud, then I can rest.* Counting each loping step, when she reached seven, the ground began to firm up under her feet.

The effort of walking through the mud left her light-headed, and the stitch in her side spread its way across her back. She balanced the gun on her thigh and used her right hand to massage her side and back. At the same time, she listened for any sounds of movement from behind her.

A gust of wind blustered against her neck and shoulders tipping her forward, making it difficult to catch her breath. She let go of her side and clutched the front of her dress. She had to keep going, if she wasted time resting, the battery in her phone would die, and then she'd be stumbling around looking for the dirt track until sunrise. *Straighten up and get moving!*

The left side of the barn was barely visible by the glow of the phone. To the right, massive swaths of trees and shrubs crowded in, their shadows drawing together to make them seem impenetrable. Paige felt tiny against the immenseness of the wilderness and the night. She stood before the thick twists of trunks and branches, defeat threatening to overtake her. Finding the entrance seemed impossible, she'd been an idiot to think she could retrace her steps and find the track using a phone light and her memory. Lizzy had chosen to hide the car on the disused dirt road because of its hidden location. She should've left something behind to mark the way. Tied something to a tree, anything.

Her mind turned to Hal, waiting for her; putting his trust in her. There was no getting around it, his life was in her hands. If she gave up, whatever ghastly things Lizzy did to him would be on Paige's shoulders. If she lived, which seemed highly doubtful, it would be with the burden of Hal's suffering. Her body trembled, and a sob burst out of her mouth. Within seconds she cried so hard, it felt like the sobs would tear her apart. She let the gun slip to the ground with a dull thump and sank down next to it.

"How the fuck did this happen?" she said around big, wet sobs.

They were on holiday in the South West. Things like this didn't really happen to people. *This is supposed to be wine country*, she thought stupidly; as if evil things couldn't grow in the same ground as grapevines.

Paige wiped at her face with the back of her hand, it came away with a mixture of tears, snot, and blood. The cut on her cheek had re-opened, she could feel it stinging but her mind barely registered the sensation. Sticks and honky nuts bit into the skin of her legs, but she remained motionless, her already grazed knees pushed into the debris carpeting the edge of the bush.

When there were no more tears, she wiped her face with the hem of her dress. The coarse fabric pulled at the graze on her cheek, bringing fresh pain and a dribble of blood. The emotions that had overwhelmed her subsided, leaving her raw with exhaustion. The phone lay on the ground between her legs. She didn't remember putting it down, but that didn't surprise her; the enormity of her situation had swallowed her up, and for a few minutes everything else disappeared. Now the reality of the dimming light hit her like a fist.

She pounced on the phone and looked at the battery indicator; almost empty. She'd wasted precious time sitting on the ground snivelling at the weight of her problems, while the only chance of finding the car was the light. Light she'd wasted.

Paige climbed to her feet, noticing the cuts and grazes on her legs for the first time. If she found the car and got the hell out of this circus, she'd have plenty of time to examine her wounds, but for now she had more important things to do. The gun felt heavier than before, its stock bulky against her body. She tried to picture the morning she'd spent with Soona; walking past the cows, past the barn, and then where? Paige screwed her face up with the effort of trying to remember.

"We came from the dam ... and then ..." She looked in what she thought was the direction of the gully dam, but could have been anything in the blackness. "Then we ..." Her mind kept telling to go past the barn, but that couldn't be right because that would walk her straight into thickly thatched trees.

Paige turned back towards the hulking outline of the barn. She closed her eyes and shut out the night so she could picture the scene in clear brilliant morning light. She saw the cows, their big black noses snuffling in the grass. Soona's back was to her as she ducked under the fence. Paige nodded to herself and moved her lips.

"I have to stop for a minute," Paige said, and her eyes sprang open.

They'd walked behind the barn and she'd had a stitch, that's why Soona went back to the cows. Paige turned to her left and headed towards the barn. She picked up the pace, not quite jogging, but definitely past walking. She reached the barn just as the wind kicked up another notch. It whipped her hair up and flattened her dress against her body. The temperature dropped fast. The wind felt like a cold hand pushing her forward. As well as propelling her, it blew the clouds to the west and the moon lit up the night. Paige gave a little cry of joy and pushed on.

The way was clearer now. The ground partially visible, the sudden change from deep green weeds to a carpet of twigs and fallen leaves revealed by the silvery moonlight. She remembered being on the far side of the barn and heading slightly to the right. She took a few more steps when the light of the torch fell on something white.

Her breath caught. She didn't believe in miracles, not the sort that opened up paths through the seas or cured the blind. Those things were no more real to her than the fairy-tales she read to her class, but the scrap of her white sundress fluttering in the wind seemed like a miracle. Maybe it wasn't a burning bush, but after the evil she'd experienced over the last four days, that scrap of fabric hanging on the spindly branch of some crazy bush shrub, clinging on despite the wind, seemed like a sign from heaven.

"We're going to make it. We're going to be okay," she said and put her hand to her belly. "Do you hear me, baby?" She felt tears on her cheeks and laughed. "I'm getting you out of here."

She pointed the phone at the bush around the strip of fabric and realised she was standing at the opening to the trail. *It's not far*, she thought and then something that had been skipping along the edges of her consciousness all afternoon clicked into place. Something Wade said just before Lizzy blew him off his motorbike. She remembered having mentioned what a long drive he had but he'd said, "It's not that f-". At the time, she'd been too horrified to take it in, but now she thought he was trying to tell her that the roadhouse wasn't far.

The shotgun grew heavier against her body, but she ignored the discomfort. The roadhouse and, more importantly, people and a phone were not far away. Her heart fluttered and her hands trembled. Could it be

159

possible that help was close by? Lizzy had said the roadhouse was a two-hour drive, *but Lizzy is a fucking lunatic.*

Paige forced herself to keep the excitement building in her chest under control. *First things first*, she reminded herself. *Get to the car.* She tucked the gun into her side and started along the trail. The looseness of the ground forced her to walk slowly and with care. Only a few steps and the smell of eucalyptus and wattle filled the air. The trees blocked out the moonlight plunging her back into almost total darkness. It didn't matter though, as long as she kept the faint blue light on the ground ahead of her and walked straight, she'd hit the Ford within minutes.

Finally things are going right for us, she thought and then another cramp hit her. This time it seized her back *and* her thighs. The pain surged up with a tremendous grip sending her lurching forward. Her mouth fell open in shock. She let the gun slip from her grasp. It hit the ground with a dry crunch. She tried to massage the pain away with her right hand, just as she'd done before. This time the cramp squeezed with an intensity she'd never experienced.

Paige took deep breaths, forcing her lungs to sweep air in and then release it in a steady pattern. The cramp loosened its grip and she started to straighten up when understanding dawned and a heavy blanket of panic covered her.

"I'm having contractions," she said into the darkness.

Chapter Twenty

Hal gave up on trying to sit. About half an hour ago the pain in his stump began became unbearable. He slid down in the bed, his broken leg grinding in protest, and put his sweat-soaked head on the pillow.

At first, he'd convinced himself the increase in pain was most likely the result of his little sailing trip to the window, but the steady pulsing in his stump told him otherwise. This new agony brought the unmistakable throbbing-burn of infection. His skin felt hot and clammy, and his mind jumpy. He could feel the infection taking hold and not in baby steps like a cut on the finger. No, this was a monster and right now, its ugly head started to rise. Pretty soon, it would lift its neck and then the snarling would begin.

He felt around under his pillow and found the scissors. The cold feel of the metal in his hand reassured his failing senses. He wrapped his fingers around the handle and drew it out; it slid against the pillowcase with a satisfying whoosh, as if he unsheathed a sword. *If I had a sword, I'd cut off the bitch's head.* That made him laugh – a chilling sound in the darkened room.

Outside the wind picked up, making the panes rattle in their crumbling putty; he was amazed they'd lasted so long in the ancient frames. For all he knew, the whole house could be consumed by wood rot. Maybe the floor would collapse under him and he'd end up in the entrance hall still lying in his bed. His thoughts became increasingly scattered. He slid the scissors under the sheets and laid them along the side of his thigh.

Satisfied they were within easy reach, he wiped his face with the edge of the sheet and focused on Paige; she'd been gone for at least forty minutes. Or had it been longer? He found it difficult to keep track of time in the dark with no watch. When she'd first left, he'd tried to count, keeping track by minutes, but by the time he reached ten, invisible screws in his stump turned ever tighter.

If it *had* been forty minutes, he had another twenty yet to wait. The thought of swinging his legs out of the bed sent cold shivers down his spine. He'd been so sure he could keep up his end of the plan. *That's before the monster woke up*, now all bets were off.

He'd never considered himself a cowardly man; he been in shit storms before his visit to Mable House. He'd done things that would terrify some people, but now thinking about getting his legs out of bed made him quake.

The mixture of cold sweats and hot fear reminded him of Afghanistan. The smell of cordite and the dry heat. There were times when he'd felt the cold fingers of terror wrap around his heart while his body remained drenched in sweat. He closed his eyes and could see the bone-coloured sand in the streets and hear the shouts. Voices raised in high pitched panic, their fear clearly recognisable even though their words were foreign.

* * *

His breathing came faster, in rough pants, like a dog too long in the sun. A little boy, a toddler in a yellow T-shirt walked towards the truck, his small legs sticking out from under long shorts like two twigs. The air felt charged and alive as if lightening might strike. The boy picked up speed, his little legs pumping, he turned to look over his shoulder at someone. Hal could see the child's face in profile; a smile lit his small chubby features and his dark hair sprang up and bounced on his small head.

Hal's eyes moved rapidly under closed lids and a moan slipped past his open lips. The boy turned back towards the truck. The vehicle was some sort of covered van, dented and crusted with sand. Hal felt the hairs on his arm rise and he called to the boy to stop. On the other side of the street – if the sandy track between rows of crumbling buildings could be called a street – the sound of empty cans tumbling into a cart rang out.

The boy reached under the truck and touched what looked like a red ball. Hal could hear himself calling for the boy to stop, but it sounded long and hollow like yelling through a tunnel. Breaking into a run, he stopped short when someone grabbed the back of his shirt and yanked. Then the blazing sun disappeared and his vision filled with orange spots, all sound sucked from the air.

When his hearing returned, sound bombarded him: metal tearing, glass shattering and, above everything, screaming. Hal tried to blink the dust out of his eyes and realised he lay on his stomach. He pushed himself to his feet and staggered forward.

"Don't mate. Don't." He heard someone say. Later he realised the warning came from Lindsey, Donald Lindsey his commanding officer. But at the time, the words made no sense. He pushed forward and his boot hit something soft, limp. He stumbled and almost fell on the body. If he hadn't pulled himself back he would have fallen and a sheet of metal, crusted with sand, would have impaled him. The jagged sheet rose out of the child's chest in a vicious point. The yellow T-shirt had been torn from his body to reveal his small torso. The child's tiny frame was almost carved in two. His skinny legs curled around at an impossible angle so that his bare feet – no bigger than Hal's thumb – almost touched his shoulder.

He heard a scream behind him, unmistakably a woman's. In the bed, Hal twisted the sheets between his hands. He didn't need to understand her words to know she was the child's mother. Her voice rose higher until her shrieking grew so loud he had to cover his ears to block out the anguish.

"Where is she? Where the fuck is she?"

* * *

Light filled the doorway and sent blazing circles of yellow spiralling in Hal's eyes. He tried to blink away the sudden blindness and make sense of what he saw. His heart pounding from the images invading his mind, made it take a few seconds for him to recognise his surroundings.

"Where is she? I'm not going to keep asking." Lizzy's voice came from the doorway. The light from the landing behind her made it impossible for Hal to see more than her outline, but the shrillness in her voice made it clear she was enraged.

Hal reached into the bed, the sheets were bunched up around his waist making it difficult for him to push his hand towards his thigh. Lizzy didn't bother with the overhead light. Either she thought she didn't need it or she'd gone past noticing that apart from the light that spilled in from the landing, the room remained dark. She stalked over to the bed, her feet pounding the boards like a military band on the move.

His fingers found the scissors, but they were the wrong way around. He fumbled to turn them and keep his hand concealed. If she saw the scissors, he'd lose the element of surprise and something told him he'd only get one chance at this.

She leaned over the bed, not close enough to grab, but within striking range. Suddenly the thought of *her* hitting *him* on his infected stump seemed worse than death. He could actually visualise the pain; it would be white. Startling and exquisitely clear white, it would swallow him up.

He twisted the scissors in his damp palm and found the handle. Her face loomed above him. A shaft of light from the door fell across her right cheek. Her eyes looked like big balls of yellow glass, shiny and bulging in their sockets. Her lips were pulled down in grimace that made her chin jut out like a cartoon witch.

"Where did she go?" She screamed with so much power, he was sure his hair blew back while the smell of sour milk covered his face.

The movement of her right arm drew his eyes away from her face. He saw her fist rise and knew what that meant. The pain would be bad, but not as bad as the other leg. He almost relaxed and let her hit away, but in that fraction of a second he saw Paige's face. Not as it was on the beach in Bali, but as it had been that afternoon – haunted, raw with fear. In that instant, he wanted to kill Lizzy. He wanted it more than he wanted to escape or find relief from the pain.

He shot his left arm out and batted down Lizzy's fist then grabbed her shoulder. He drew her into him. Her mouth opened in a circle of surprise and a rush of air blew out. She fell forward, her doughy bosoms mashed against his chest.

"Let go!" Her voice sounded uncharacteristically high-pitched and panicky.

Hal would never admit it, but her fear pleased him more than he cared to acknowledge. He pulled the scissors from under the sheet with his right hand and stabbed them into Lizzy's neck. He felt them cut through skin and hit something solid. She gave an ear-piercing screech but continued to struggle.

He could feel her right arm pushing against his thighs and knew if he didn't stop her, blows would rain down on his legs. He pulled the scissors out of her flesh and heard a ripping sound like an old sheet tearing in half.

"Stop! Stop." Her screams turned into words and Hal knew he'd missed the mark on her neck.

Lizzy's right hand slapped his stomach and the air rushed out of his lungs. She seized the opportunity and pulled away.

"No you don't, you fucking bitch." The words came out of his mouth, but he didn't recognise the pitiless cruelty.

He stabbed at her a second time, the blades cutting through flesh with a wet slurp and hitting bone. Lizzy howled. She arched her back and pulled out of his grasp almost taking him off the bed in the process. Hal felt his backside rise off the mattress and then bump back down with a thud. The pain flowed through his legs like an electric shock.

He held onto the scissors and could feel his hand covered in a sticky wet substance. From the doorway Lizzy heaved laboured breaths. She leaned against the frame with her back to him. The landing light illuminated her left side. A rapidly spreading stain turned her shirt dark red. The blood flowed fast, but it was obviously not arterial or it would've spurted like a fountain.

He held the scissors up. The strength he'd used to pull Lizzy down had dissipated and his hand shook. If she took another run at him, he didn't think he could stop her. Instead of attacking, she pushed herself off the door frame and staggered onto the landing. He could hear a door opening and what sounded like a tray hitting the floor.

The image of her holding the hacksaw flashed before his eyes. He moaned. *Will she get a weapon and come back for me?* No, he'd stabbed her twice, *she's crazy, not Superwoman.* Both times, the scissors had gone deep, he'd driven them in with enough force to know they done some damage. She wouldn't come back. If he was lucky, she'd collapse from loss of blood and die. *If I was lucky, I wouldn't be sitting*

166

here with one leg, he thought, and a dry gurgle somewhere between a laugh and a sob passed through his cracked lips.

He didn't have time to ponder Lizzy's next move, he had to get going. When she'd burst into his room, she'd been so enraged that Paige had dared slip away without her knowledge, she didn't notice the wheelchair sitting to the right side of his bed. If she noticed during their wrestling match, she'd kept it to herself.

The chair was from the nineteen seventies, with a leather seat and big wheels. Hal reached out and grabbed the arm of it, pulling it alongside the bed. The wheels squeaked like a guinea pig. *This is it.* The part he'd been afraid of. Somehow slamming his ass into the old chair seemed more terrifying than facing a mad woman intent on chopping him up into little pieces. Or maybe what really scared him had nothing to do with pain. It was failure that terrified him. Letting Paige down when she needed help, because losing his leg really did make him less of a man.

On the landing, footsteps sounding heavy but slower than before, creaked past the door. Hal held up the scissors and waited. He heard a metallic clang and then a whirring sound as if something mechanical was winding up. His first thought, a chainsaw, and his feverish mind grasped onto it. His heart jackhammered in his chest as his ears filled with rushing blood.

He threw the sheets back and turned the wheelchair so the seat faced him and then inched his body to the edge of the bed. All the while he listened to the whirring and clanking, waiting for Lizzy to appear in the doorway.

The first attempt to swing his butt into the chair was a misfire; in his panic, he tried to lean his arms on the seat and pull himself forward, which tipped the chair and nearly sent him nose-diving to the floor. By the time he'd pulled the chair back in place, the whirring had stopped and an echoing clang came from downstairs. *The lift,* he realised. A shudder of relief passed through him.

The relief was short lived. The lift meant that Lizzy was still on the move. Maybe not able to tackle three flights of stairs, but she definitely had something in mind. Whether that something would be for him or Paige, he didn't know. He *did* know he needed to get his ass in the chair and get going.

This time, he slid the wheelchair seat under his bed so the arms were nearly touching the top of the mattress. He used his hip and slid his infected leg over the side of the bed. With his stump in mid-air, he bent his knee and balanced on the edge of the bed with one butt cheek.

With his ass half in and half out of the bed, a wave of wooziness washed over him. For one horrifying second he thought he'd pass out. Shaking his head sent drops of sweat across the bed before he snapped his eyes open and closed. It was as if someone had smeared Vaseline on them, blurring his vision. *Come on, come on*, came the chant over and over in his head.

The sloppy vision and the wooziness only lasted a couple of seconds, and then the room returned to focus. Hal knew another wave could hit him at any time, better to be firmly in the chair than hanging out of bed. He stuffed the scissors in the top pocket of his old-man pyjamas and dropped his right hand onto the arm of the wheelchair. After a few seconds of grunting and shifting, he firmly planted his ass in place.

Downstairs, a door slammed. The sound had a distant quality, as if it had come from the back of the house. Hal's eyes opened wide, he paused and listened. He thought he heard a distant creak, the sound of footsteps on the back porch. Is that what he'd heard or had his imagination supplied the sound? Then another creak, louder than the last and most definitely real. He hoisted his broken leg on to the footrest and groaned through the sheet of pain that spiralled under his shin.

It had to have been Lizzy on the back stairs, which meant she was going after Paige. Hal pulled the brake release and used both hands to wheel himself around the bed. He had to get to the lift and make it downstairs. He hoped he'd done enough damage to Lizzy's neck to slow her down and give Paige time to get to the car.

Chapter Twenty-One

Paige dug her nails into the bark of a broad gum tree and let out a series of curses. The swearing turned into panting that came out through hot, damp lips. Mercifully, the giant fists that squeezed her lower body loosened their grip. Not all at once, but slowly as if resenting letting her go.

"Holy Christ." Paige walked her hands up the trees until she pulled herself upright.

Why now? The car was within view; the silvery-grey moonlight crept through the gaps in the canopy and lit up the vehicle in dusty stripes. All she had to do was walk ten metres and get in. *Just another minute and then I'll do it*, Paige promised herself.

Her breathing evened out and after a few halting breaths, returned to near normal. The wind died down; it ruffled the hair on the back of her neck with a cool burst. She pushed off the tree and crouched sideways to where the shotgun sat at her feet. *Drive to the roadhouse and send help back for Hal*, the dark voice spoke up.

Paige shook her head. "I'm not going without Hal."

If you die, the baby dies. The voice, flat and unemotional replied. Paige gritted her teeth and kept walking. She tried using the shotgun as a crutch. Her steps were short and faltering as if she were drunk and the barrel kept jerking sideways throwing her off balance. She hoisted the weapon back up to her hip. *I can do it, just a bit farther.* All she had to do was get to the car. The contractions were at least fifteen minutes apart and Wade had said the roadhouse wasn't that far.

I can get Hal and make it to the roadhouse before the baby comes. It occurred to Paige that she spoke to herself, but her mental health was the least of her problems.

The voice in her head remained silent, at least for the time being. For that, she was grateful. The car beckoned to her, almost within touching distance. She could see the film of dirt on the back window and in a few seconds, she'd be behind the wheel. The best part would be putting the shotgun on the seat next to her. Carrying it had been awkward enough, but now it felt like it weighed twenty kilos of sharp edges.

Paige leaned her shoulder against the back passenger door as much for reassurance as support. Until she touched it, she almost expected the car to waver and disappear like a cartoon mirage in the desert. She let lose a small cry of triumph and somewhere to her left a bird shrieked and took flight. The undergrowth continued to rustle as though the bird had set off an entire flock.

Paige ignored the movement and slid her way along the Ford. Her tennis shoes crunched on the bed of dried leaves surrounding the vehicle and the barrel of the gun trailed close to the ground. The battery signal on the phone turned red and the light flickered out.

"Great timing." Inside the tunnel of bush and overgrown grass trees, her voice sounded thick and disembodied.

She pulled open the driver's door and the internal light encircled her in a yellowy glow. She patted the pocket on her dress and felt the comforting bulge of the keys.

"Almost …"

Arms, thick and strong, gripped her shoulders and pulled her back. She cried out in shock but the sound was lost in the scuffle. Paige tried to pull away, but the fingers that gripped the flesh between her shoulders and armpits were like talons.

"No! You're not taking the baby away from me, not again." Lizzy's voice was guttural.

Paige worked her shoulders in a circle and managed to pull her right arm free. She felt a hand in her hair and her head snapped back with enough force to tear strands out. Paige gasped and pulled against the hand, the back of her head hot, as if on fire. She managed to lean forward and get some leverage. She put her weight on her left foot and kicked back with her right.

The blow connected with Lizzy's shin and Paige heard a croak. The woman released her hair, maybe to grab hold somewhere else, but Paige didn't wait to find out. She turned with the shotgun still clasped to her side. As she came around, Lizzy lunged forward, her hands reaching for Paige's neck.

Paige brought the barrel of the gun up and heard a crack. Lizzy howled and dropped her right arm. She staggered back a step giving Paige the room she needed to get the shotgun between her and Lizzy. *Do it*, the dark voice urged, sounding excited.

Lizzy stopped moving and cradled her right elbow in her left hand. Her face pulled into a grimace and her salt and pepper hair stood up like wild-fire on her scalp. Paige tried to speak, but her throat contracted and nothing came out. For a few terrifying seconds, the two women regarded each other. The only sound came from the wind slipping through the trees and their combined breathing: Paige's fast and deep, Lizzy's laboured and halting.

"Stay back or I'll shoot." Paige finally got her throat working.

Lizzy's eyes were huge and glassy, flickering between the barrel of the shotgun and Paige's face.

"I just want to help you. You're in labour, aren't you?"

Paige kept the gun trained on her. She wasn't sure how Lizzy knew about her labour, but the only thing that mattered was getting Hal and the baby to safety.

"Get …" She meant to warn Lizzy, tell her to back away, but stopped. She noticed the dressings on her shoulder. Paige could see the edges, white and secured with tape visible above the woman's collar. Blood coated Lizzy's shirt. In some areas it looked dry and brown. Around the collar wet blood stuck to the dressing.

"What happened to your shoulder?" Paige asked, already knowing the answer.

"It's nothing." Lizzy stopped nursing her elbow and pulled on her collar. "Let me help you. Give me the keys and I'll drive us back to the house. I've helped deliver hundreds of babies." Lizzy's tone softened. "If you don't let me help, you'll be risking your life and the baby's."

"Get back," Paige bit off the words. "Step away from me."

Lizzy ignored her and reached out her hand. "I'll drive you and the baby to the roadhouse, I promise. Just put the gun down and let me help." Lizzy's voice lost the soft coaxing tone and become more demanding. Her skin looked grey, like an over-boiled egg yolk and her mouth puckered.

"Get back or I'll shoot." Paige could feel the giant hand closing around her middle and the cold sweat forming on her upper lip. She forced her face to remain still, resisting the urge to groan.

"You can't fool me," Lizzy said in the supercilious tone she used when smashing eggs on Soona's forehead. "You're having a contraction right now, aren't you, ducky?" Lizzy took a step forward and put her hand on the barrel of the gun.

Paige could feel the barrel dip towards the ground. In a few seconds, she'd be so far in the grip of the contraction, she'd drop the gun completely. Lizzy smiled and her upper teeth appeared like a row of fence posts in a field of flesh. Paige laced her fingers around the trigger and gritted her teeth.

Lizzy took hold of the barrel and began to pull the shotgun out of Paige's hands. Instinctively, Paige pulled back and the butt of the gun hit her in the belly. Fire exploded in Paige's abdomen and she let out a howl that came from deep in her lungs.

Lizzy let go of the gun and covered her mouth with her hands. "Oh no. Oh no."

Paige leaned back in the open door of the Ford and hit her back against the side of the driver's seat. She felt another spiral of pain in the middle of her back and cried out like a terrified dog about to be kicked. Her hands clenched and the shotgun blasted in her hands. The gun jerked back and the butt of the weapon hit her in the stomach a second time.

Paige dropped like a slab of meat on the butcher's block. Her butt hit the ground first with a teeth-jarring jolt, then her body slumped to the left. Dark blotches floated in front of her eyes. Her last thoughts before losing consciousness were of Hal and the way he smiled over his sunglasses and touched her belly. She moved her lips to say his name, but before the word formed, the world went black.

Chapter Twenty-Two

Hal clamped his hands on the thick rubber and pushed the wheels forward. The antique chair squealed and rolled towards the door. With each forward push of his arms, his leg thumped in pain, which covered him in sweat and made his head swim. Streams of sweat dripped through his brows and into his eyes. He paused long enough to lift his pyjama shirt and wipe his face. When his vision cleared, he pushed on.

The wheelchair looked like a museum piece and sounded like a dying cat, but it still had some grunt to it. Hal made it out of the bedroom and across the landing quicker than he would've guessed.

Even before he pulled up in front of the lift, he could see the housing was empty. The cage still sat on the ground floor where Lizzy had left it.

"You don't make things easy," he said to the empty housing.

He pushed the brass button with an arrow pointing upwards. The lift came to life with a shudder and groaned its way up. Hal wheeled backwards away from the housing and turned the chair in a tight circle. It took two attempts to bring the wheels around so that he faced the metal gate.

By the time the footrests were lined up with the entrance, Hal's vision whirred in time with the progress of the ancient lift.

A wave of nausea sprang up from his middle and before he'd had time to do more than turn his head to the side, a thick volley of vomit spilled from his mouth. *I'm being poisoned. That rusty hacksaw did a real job on me and now the infection's eating me up. She didn't even wash her fucking hands.* Another wave of sickness hit him, it caught him unprepared and instead of vomiting over the side of the chair, the stream of yellowish fluid fell in his lap.

The lift clanked to a stop in front of him. He reached out and pulled the door open, his arm quivered and flopped forward. His eyelids fluttered and the lift seemed to lurch towards him.

"Holy shit," he mumbled and his head dropped forward.

I just need to stop for a second, he told himself and then slumped sideways. He wasn't unconscious, nor fully awake. He was aware of sounds, like the shuffling of feet and the creaking of the stairs. He could smell the vomit in his lap, acrid and cloying. In his mind, he could see the monster: its long bumpy neck raising high, and its pale grey eyes like enormous balloons. It moved its reptilian head from side to side and Hal knew it was getting ready to roar. When it did, the pain would send him out of his mind or kill him. The later seemed the most appealing option.

"Shhhh," Hal whispered through feverish lips and the monster closed its mouth and regarded him with those grey balloon eyes. "Shhhh," he said again, and it lowered its head.

His chin felt glued to his chest; it took a gargantuan effort to pull it free and raise his head. Hal groaned and his head wobbled like a dashboard figure on an off-road joy ride. He contemplated pulling the lift door open when he heard a booming crack – the sound distant, yet sharp and clear. Even in his fevered mind, it registered as a gunshot.

"Paige." It came out as a whisper.

His mind tried to work through the possibilities. Had Paige shot Lizzy or had the mad woman got the gun away from his wife? He grabbed for the lift door. At first his hand closed around thin air and his arm slid into his lap. His depth perception was off kilter. Ignoring the vomit that clung to his wrist, he tried again and felt the cold steel in his grasp.

Swallowing another wave of nausea, he worked the handle. The door shook and then moved sideways, its progress painfully slow. His breath came through his teeth making a *fuhh* sound. With the door open, the interior of the lift yawned like a dark tunnel. *How could a lift be that big?*

The wheels were in his hands, but the chair wouldn't move. *I'm stuck. I'm stuck and Paige needs me.* His mind tried to make sense of why he wasn't moving. He pushed down on the thick rubber and his hands slipped forward. The pain in his stump eclipsed the grinding in his broken leg. It filled his head until all he could see was pulsing light. Tears trickled down his flaming cheeks and a raspy sob broke out of his mouth.

His shoulders slumped and his face quivered. Even if he could get downstairs, what good would it do? Paige was somewhere outside in the dark and he could never hope to reach her. In that moment, he gave himself permission to give up. *She's better off on her own now anyway.* He let his hands dangle at the sides of the wheelchair. He tilted his head forward and listened to the whimpering sounds coming from his mouth.

Only, *his* lips weren't moving and the whimpering got louder. Hal raised his head half expecting to be hurt in some way. Lizzy would be standing over him and this time she would use the hacksaw on his neck. A small part of him almost hoped she'd be there to finish him off. Anything, just so long as the pain and fear ended.

Vision distorted, he could make out the silhouette of someone near the chair. "Get it over with. Just don't hurt Paige."

When nothing happened, Hal's frenzied mind cleared. Not all the way, just enough for him to blink his eyes and try to focus. A woman stood beside his chair. He took in her face and large frame.

"Help me?" He croaked. "Help me, Soona?"

The mewling ceased and the wheelchair moved forward into the lift. The door to the cage clanged shut behind him. With a *clunk* the lift descended. For the first time in four days, Hal left the third floor of Mable House.

Chapter Twenty-Three

Paige tasted something in her mouth. Dry and gritty, it reminded her of falling off the monkey bars when she was in year three. She'd landed on her stomach and the wind had been knocked out of her like her tummy was a paper bag that had been blown up and then popped. She'd opened her mouth to cry, but couldn't get enough breath out, instead she sucked in a mouthful of sand.

She raised her hand to wipe the grit out of her mouth and heard crunching in her ear. She opened her eyes and winced at the bright light that shone down on her. The car door came into focus and she became aware of her surroundings. With awareness came panic. Instinctively her hand went to her belly and found the bump. *I shot her. I shot Lizzy and the kickback hit me in the stomach*, the memory of gun in her hands, and the tearing pain when the butt jerked, flooded back like a bad dream.

Grunting and struggling, she pushed herself into a sitting position. Something crunched against her ear. She touched her hand to the side of her face and pulled away dried leaves, crumbling them and letting the bits fall into her lap. Her body felt strangely pain free or maybe she was too numb to feel anything.

The driver's door stood open and the light from the car's interior circled her. She wanted to stand, but didn't trust her legs enough yet. Before her mind had time to formulate questions, she saw Lizzy's shoes. Rubber soles visible in the outer circle of the light. The shoes were sitting at an almost perfect right angle, toes pointing skywards. *I blew her out of her shoes*, Paige thought crazily. For a second it seemed plausible, until she heard the noises and realised the shoes were attached to legs.

"Huck ... Heek."

One shoe moved and slid out to the left, dragging crackling leaves behind the heel as a boat drags white water. The sight of that foot sliding its way across the dirt track got Paige moving. She grabbed the wheel arch on the driver's side of the Ford and pulled herself into a crouching position. She was aware of a wet slippery sound. Above her knees where her dress had ridden up, she saw blood on her thighs. *No. No, the baby's okay. That's my blood.* Yes, the baby had to be okay. If she could just get help *everything* would still be okay.

She managed to stand by clinging onto the open door. She winced at the pulling sensation in her abdomen, it felt like the muscles had shrunk and were being stretched. Now upright, she could see Lizzy sprawled on her back. The woman's head moved, tilted up and fixed her gaze on Paige. In the shadows, Lizzy's eyes looked like empty sockets and her cheeks bleached white by the edges of the light. For a moment, they regarded each other.

"D... don't take my b... baby." A singed area on the right arm of Lizzy's shirt, just above the elbow revealed the impact of the shot. The fabric was shredded in blackened strips and the skin underneath looked dark and wet.

When Paige pulled the trigger, the shot must have clipped her, peppering her upper arm with tiny lead pellets. *Finish her off*, the dark voice ordered, and Paige's eyes fell on the shotgun a metre or so away. It lay half buried in leaves. It was empty, she knew, yet for a second she considered picking it up and bashing the woman's head in with the butt. She even managed to conjure up the satisfying crack the heavy wooden stock would make when it split Lizzy's skull open. *Do it or she'll come after you.*

Paige moved forward, she didn't think she could bend from the waist so she crouched down and picked up the shotgun. The stretching sensation in her belly came again only this time it was accompanied by a shaft of heat in her groin.

Lizzy's leg shuffled through the leaves and drew up towards her body. Her gaze still fixed on Paige, she raised herself up on her left shoulder and flipped onto her side. She dragged herself towards the trees. Paige couldn't see the woman's eyes, only the dark sockets as they looked over her shoulder.

Paige advanced on Lizzy, the barrel clenched in her hands. *Hit her, put an end to it; it'll never be over while she's still alive,* the urgency in the voice edged on excitement, encouraging her to stop the nightmare once and for all.

"Don't. Don't." Lizzy's voice was high and wavered with fear.

Paige swung the butt of the gun and knocked Lizzy's right arm out from under her. The woman splayed forward, her face hitting the track in a spray of twigs and gravel. Paige fixed her eyes on the back of Lizzy's scalp and raised the gun over her head. *One last hurdle. One last thing to do and then everything would be quiet,* Paige told herself.

She would've done it. She would have killed the woman who'd driven her past pain and past humanity to the edge of reason where the only thing that made sense was brutality. But at the last minute, just before Paige brought the butt of the gun down on the woman's head, Lizzy flipped over. The moonlight landed on the woman's face and drove the shadows out of her eyes. What was left was fear and madness, a fretful shifting, pitiful and frightening at the same time.

The dark voice urged Paige on, but the excitement had dissipated turning it into nothing more than a hollow echo. Paige lowered the gun and saw Lizzy flinch. The fear on her tormentor's face gave her no pleasure or satisfaction, just a numb distaste for Lizzy and herself.

"Stay down." The flinty growl in those two words made Lizzy flinch again.

Paige turned and walked back to the car. When she reached the driver's side, she realized the shotgun was still in her hands. Repulsed by the feel of it against her skin *and* what she'd almost down with it, Paige tossed it onto the track and pulled herself up onto the seat. The heat in her groin remained, making every other feeling seem distant and unimportant.

The car started the first time. Paige felt neither joy nor relief, just a fatigue seeping all the way to her bones. She clicked the headlights on and the Ford rolled forward, loose stones and twigs crunching under the wheels. She glanced in the wing mirror and saw Lizzy sitting with her head in her hands. The woman's reflection grew smaller and then darkness enveloped her. Paige looked back at the track and flicked the headlights to high.

Chapter Twenty-Four

"We need to get outside." Hal pointed at the front door and looked back over his shoulder. The foyer sat mostly in darkness except for the light from the other side of the sitting room. He guessed it came from the kitchen.

Soona swayed from left to right and then shuffled around the wheelchair towards the door. She seemed reluctant to touch the handle, her hand fluttered towards it and then back as though it was too hot to touch.

"I need to get outside. Paige is coming for me and I have to be out front." Hal didn't know if the woman understood what he was saying or if his words were even coming out coherently. A blanket of sweat covered his body and his lungs felt as if they were being squeezed. The thought of being outside with the cool night air touching his skin seemed as appealing as leaving the house.

"Please, Soona, just open the door?"

The woman was dressed in men's blue striped pyjamas, very similar to the ones Lizzy had put on Hal after the amputation. It occurred to him that the two of them looked like they were escapees from a mental hospital. He would've laughed if it hadn't been so close to the truth *and* if his lungs didn't feel like someone held a naked flame under them.

"Open the door," he croaked, hoping a simplified instruction might be more effective.

Soona mumbled something that sounded a bit like, "Don't touch" and turned the handle. The door swept inwards and a gentle breeze played over Hal's face. Like plunging into a swimming pool on a stinking hot day, the cold shocked him at first and then brought sweet relief. The air smelled fresh and clear, tinged with the sour smell of vomit rising up from his lap.

"Good girl." It came out as a gasp. He was finding it difficult to catch his breath. "You did … good. Wheel me … out."

Soona didn't need any more prompting, she hustled back to the chair and wheeled him over the doorstep. The wheels bumped and a shaft of pain rocketed up his leg before jumping behind his eyes. He groaned as a wave of nausea hit. He retched a few times but nothing came out.

The wheelchair stalled just outside the house, and as his eyes adjusted to the moonlight he saw they were on a raised veranda. Just how high up was difficult to tell. *How the fuck am I going to get down,* he thought and his head began to drop forward again.

A light flickered on overhead. The sudden brightness of its glare snapped him back to awareness. Soona grabbed the handles of the wheelchair and turned him to the left. He could see the enormous wrap-around veranda jutted at least two and a half metres off the ground. He experienced a moment of panic, imagining Soona taking him down a flight of stairs one painful drop-step at a time.

He opened his mouth to tell her to stop so he could prepare himself for the frightening descent when Hal realised she was pushing him down the long, gentle slope of a ramp. If he had the strength, he would've turned around and kissed one of Soona's large hands.

"Good girl. Good girl." It was the best he could do.

Chapter Twenty-Five

The headlights bounced across a tightly-packed cluster of shrubs that looked as sharp as Christmas holly but ghostly grey in colour. Paige kept the speedometer on thirty to avoid the bone-crunching dips and gouges in the old track and so that she could keep the twin ruts that marked the track in sight. Outside the orbs of light, the trees crowded out the moonlight and murky darkness surrounded the vehicle. Even with the windows up the chatter of insects and the occasional eerie calls of night birds seemed to close in on her.

The house had to be on the right of the track, and judging by the way the ruts swept to the east, she was pretty sure she was travelling in an arc that would bring her out somewhere near the front driveway. At least she hoped that's what would happen. If she had it wrong and she ended up at a dead end … Her thinking faltered, what then? *I'll reverse.* It sounded good in theory, but she wasn't sure she would be physically capable of turning in her seat and guiding the four-wheel-drive all the way back. Not to mention searching the almost black wilderness for another track.

She tried to keep her mind from contemplating her physical state. She didn't want to think about the absence of movement in her belly or that she hadn't had a contraction since before the gun hit her in the stomach. And she *really* didn't want to think about the blood on her thighs and the warm wetness under her ass. Paige narrowed her thoughts until the only things she could see were the ruts ahead of the headlights.

Less than five minutes later, the track sloped up slightly and the ruts ended at a gravel road. Paige let out a long shaky breath and braked. Blackness in both directions. She leaned her head on the wheel and closed her eyes. It had to be right, that was the only way that made sense. Only out here in the dark, nothing seemed normal. She lifted her head and made a decision.

"Please God, let this be right," she muttered and turned.

Tiny stones and specks of gravel pelted the car with a constant thwack. The continuous irritating sound fed Paige's feeling of panic. Something was wrong. *You're being ridiculous*, she told herself. For the last four days, everything had been so far from right, she didn't even know what right was anymore. But the gnawing feeling ate its way up her throat until she felt like she had a peach stone stuck in the back of her mouth.

The road swelled upwards and then dipped. Paige recognised the rise and fall; she remembered experiencing the same motion sitting in the bed of the old Holden. She'd had her hand on Hal's chest trying to reassure herself that he was still breathing. Plenty of roads dipped and rose, but Paige had no doubt she was near Mable House. A flutter of anticipation awakened in her chest.

Within seconds of recognising the terrain, a light appeared as if out of nowhere. Paige drove forward, eyes wide and mouth set in a grim line. She looked very little like the woman who'd sat in the bed of the ute clinging to her husband.

186

The headlights picked out the main entrance, lighting up the weathered stone steps and a few metres of veranda. She leaned forward scanning the porch for any sign of Hal. Paige turned the wheel, the Ford veered to the right and sailed off the gravel. The old Holden ute blocked the side of the house like a giant alien bug, hulking and immoveable.

Paige jerked the gearstick into park with a fierce grunt and opened the door. She slid down from the driver's seat and wobbled drunkenly to her right. Her legs felt like overstuffed bags of sand wanting to fold on themselves. She held the side of the open door for support and forced herself to remain still so she could listen. The wind had dropped to little more than an occasional puff, and beyond the chirp of insects the outside of the house was still. She doubted Lizzy would've made it back to the house. When she'd last seen her, the woman looked defeated; yet Paige's heart drummed against her rib cage and the skin on her arms broke out in goose bumps.

It's just being back here, she told herself and let go of the door. A squealing came from the front end of the ute. Paige tensed. Her whole body reacted to the noise: her heart missed a beat and her gut clenched. She took a step backwards and felt for the knife in her pocket, silently praying she had enough strength left to use it.

Something appeared low to the ground ahead of the ute's front right tyre. The tyre and the object were just beyond the field of the Ford's headlights. Paige had a startling vision of Lizzy crawling all the way back from the dirt track on her hands and knees. Her shirt ragged with grime, drenched in blood, and her mouth hanging open in a hungry snarl. The image, eerily vivid, forced her to pull the knife from her pocket and hold it in front of her.

A dragging squeal followed by a thump issued from the far end of the car. Paige's face trembled with the combination of fear and weakness. The knife waved from side to side, her hand battled to keep a steady grip on the handle. *No more, please. I don't think I can take any more,* she thought or said; she wasn't sure which.

The wheelchair emerged from the shadow of the ute. Hal slumped in the seat, head on his chest and hands in his lap. Paige's eyes moved from Hal to Soona. She didn't realise she was moving, yet somehow Paige was in front of the wheelchair – touching her husband's hair.

He remained unmoving and slumped. Paige drew her hand back, *was she too late?* He looked shrunken and lifeless.

Paige put her hand on his face and the heat coming from him was both a relief and a jolt. His skin burned with fever.

"Hal?" She pushed his hair back and pressed her lips to his forehead. "Hal, I made it."

Slowly, an almost imperceptible movement, his chin lifted and his eyes opened. A husky breath escaped his lips.

"I never doubted you," he croaked, and the corner of his mouth twitched as if he were about to smile.

He lost consciousness again so quickly, Paige wondered if he'd really spoken. She could hear him breathing now, shallow and laboured as if there was something in his throat blocking the flow of air.

"Soona, help me get him in the car."

Soona's big brown eyes met Paige's for less than a second and then drifted away. The woman's hands tightened on the handles of the wheelchair and she began pushing it forward towards the Ford.

"Quick," Paige said over her shoulder as she pulled the back passenger door open. "Help me get him in the back."

Soona grabbed Hal under the arms and locked her hands around his chest. She hauled him up and out of the chair with a guttural grunt. She stood for a moment, backing into the car with Hal dangling like a scarecrow in her arms. Paige hesitated, in awe of the woman's strength.

"Its eyes are balloons," Hal muttered and then groaned.

The pain in her husband's voice snapped her attention back to the urgency of the matter. Paige slid one hand around Hal's ankle and used the other to grasp just above the bloody bandage on his severed leg. She tried to touch him as gently as possible, only guiding his legs over the wheel arch and into the car. But it seemed no matter how she held his legs, he jerked and groaned in her hands.

"I'm sorry, Hal. Not much more. It's nearly over." At the sound of his name, Hal's eyes snapped open and the frenzied look in them cut through her heart. The rawness and confusion was more terrifying than the searing heat coming off his skin.

Soona slid backwards across the seat, arms still locked around Hal's chest. When she reached the far door, she hoisted his head across her lap and patted his forehead.

"Thank you, sweetheart," Paige leaned into the back seat. "Thank you for helping us." She wanted to say more, but Soona's big dark eyes drifted away from her.

Paige wouldn't allow her eyes to linger on Hal. The thick raspy sound of his breathing was enough to tell her they were running out of time. She reversed herself out of the back seat and closed the door with a *thunck*. Wobbling towards the driver's door, she managed to climb back in. With her husband in the car, she felt her body running out of strength. The heat in her groin spread to her lower abdomen with an intensity that threatened to blossom into a full-blown fire.

She put the Ford in reverse. Turning in her seat was nearly impossible so she craned her neck and backed away from the house. When the tyres hit gravel, she moved the gearstick back into drive and turned in a wide arc. In the rear-view mirror, Mable House looked like a colossal grey monster rising up to snatch the car and suck them all back into its belly. Paige almost expected the house to pull out of its foundations and thunder towards them, dragging the veranda behind it like a long, cracked tongue.

That didn't happen. The Ford crackled over the gravel and within a minute, the house shrank to a distant spot of yellow light. Paige lowered the window a crack and let the night air whistle through the car. In the back seat, she could hear Hal's laboured breathing. *Whatever happens now, at least we won't die in that house.*

The dense bush flew by in a crowded rush of silver and black. Cold air blasted through the window blowing her hair back off her face. After four days of stagnation, Paige felt like she was flying. The stars were startling spots of light against the velvet night. She glanced over her shoulder. Soona held Hal's head cradled in her lap, patting his hair as if he were a kitten. His pale face glowed in the dim of the car as if it had been stained with grey reflective paint. *He's dying*, Paige thought, and resisted the urge to pull over and wrap herself around his frail body.

She looked back at the road and caught sight of a dark blur dart out of the trees. She reacted instinctively, hitting the brake pedal without thinking. The Ford skidded, losing traction on the loose dirt and rocks that blanketed the road. For a millisecond, it seemed to leave the road and float above the bitumen as if it were flying. Paige took her foot off the brake and then stomped it back down. This time the wheels caught and the car shuddered to a stop, jarring her forward. The seatbelt snapped back across her belly sending a fresh dagger of pain burning, not on the surface, but deep in her womb.

A curtain of mist played in front of Paige's eyes and her head tipped to the left. She felt her hands slipping off the wheel. *I'm blacking out*, she felt no alarm in the thought just surprise. Her jaw felt loose and her lips numb, as if she'd just come from the dentist. She was aware of Soona's voice, it sounded echoey and distant. Paige tried to understand what she was saying, but the effort seemed too great. *Easier to just rest*, her mind told her. And then a tingling sensation spread through her arms and legs, the feeling not unpleasant just foreign. She wanted to fold into

190

the feeling and let it smother her with warmth. *If only the noise would stop*, Paige thought. *If it was quiet, I could rest ... Just for a minute.*

"Paige." Hal's voice, pained and desperate broke through the blackness.

Paige's eyes flew open. Her vision was dark and grainy. For a second, she thought she'd gone blind and panic gripped her. Then, the feel of the steering wheel against her forehead and the pull of the belt across her body told her she was slumped forward looking at the steering column.

"Paige, are you hurt?" Hal's voice from the back seat was urgent yet weak.

She drew in a breath and shivered. The air from the open window, blessedly cool on her neck and cheek. Paige pulled her head back and sat up in the seat. It took her a moment to understand what she was seeing. Fifteen metres ahead on the road, surely no more than twenty, the thing that had stumbled out of the trees crouched in the road.

"Paige?" Hal's voice faded away to a whisper.

"I'm okay," she muttered, her eyes fixed on the thing in the road.

Even before the shape unfolded itself and stood, Paige knew with discomforting clarity that it was Lizzy. She knew, with a deep certainty that coiled itself around her heart like a black hand, it wasn't over.

The dark mass lurched up and forward, coming into the arc of the car's lights. Her face, a loose mask lined with blood, showed red streaks that looked as dark as oil in the yellow glare. Lizzy listed to one side, her shoulder hanging at an impossible angle. Her clothes bloody and torn, she was barely recognisable as human except for her eyes. Those bulging shark-eyes shone in the moonlight like huge, watery, glass balls.

"Everything's okay, Hal," Paige said absently, her gaze fixed on Lizzy.

The engine ticked rhythmically and the sound of insects chirping out night calls drifted in through the open window. Lizzy raised her left arm and held it in front of her, palm up, fingers curled towards the night sky. It almost looked like she was asking for help, but Paige knew better.

"Don't touch. Don't touch," Soona began to shriek.

Lizzy moved forward. Even over Soona's cries, Paige could hear the sensible rubber soled shoes sliding across the road. The woman's mouth opened and closed, mouthing words. Not *help*. No, even from ten metres away, Paige could see the same word forming over and over on Lizzy's lips: *baby*.

It's not over. It'll never be over. Lizzy was like an unstoppable machine and she meant to have what she thought belonged to her. Paige realised that some part of her had known what she had to do all along. Maybe even from the moment she picked up the phone in Lizzy's kitchen and heard that flat empty silence.

"Soona," Paige said as gently as she could manage. "I want you to close your eyes. Can you do that?"

Soona's breathing, loud and frightened, levelled off. "Eyes. Eyes."

"That's right, sweetheart. Close your eyes and don't open them until I tell you to."

As she spoke, she kept her gaze trained on Lizzy – now less than five metres in front of the car. Within seconds, the woman would close the gap and be upon them. Paige felt another wave of dizziness threatening to sweep her away.

If she let Lizzy get to the car, it would be over. Paige didn't have the strength left to fight her. She clenched her teeth and jerked the gearstick into reverse. As her foot found the accelerator, she felt wetness, warm and sticky spreading against her thighs.

"Hang on, please," Paige whispered, and the car rolled back.

Lizzy's progress faltered, but didn't stop. Through the windscreen, Paige could see the woman's eyes fixed on her. Huge glassy eyes. There was no pain in those eyes, just fury.

"Keep your eyes closed, sweetheart. It's nearly over."

Lizzy closed the gap fast, her arm still reaching for the car. Paige stomped the accelerator and the Ford's wheels spun. For one terrible second, it seemed the vehicle refused to move. Then, as if some invisible cord had been cut, the car shot forward.

Lizzy's face seemed to grow and expand until it filled Paige's vision. The woman's mouth continued to open and close as if she were oblivious to the four-wheel-drive bearing down on her. The image of Hal's leg washed beyond white under the water flashed in Paige's mind. At the last moment, Lizzy threw herself forward.

Gravel and sticks pelted the sides of the car. At the moment of impact, a dull thud followed by a slapping sound shook the vehicle. Lizzy's body jack-knifed forward and her legs seemed to bend up behind her as if she were executing an elaborate summersault. Her face neared the windscreen for no longer than a fraction of a second. Long enough for Paige to see the confusion and terror in her eyes. An image that Paige knew she'd take with her and see again and again in her nightmares.

Lizzy's body looked like it was being swallowed by the car. She slid backwards, mouth open like a black cave. One arm slapped the bonnet then her salt and pepper hair vanished over the front end of the car. The right side of the Ford lifted and then snapped back to the road with a cracking sound.

The crunching and slapping continued for less than two seconds and then the night returned to its former song. Paige blinked, her eyes felt dry and pasted open. *What've I done?* Her mind screamed. *What you should have done three days ago*, the dark voice answered. *No*, Paige thought. *That's not right. That's not me. I'm not a killer ... Am*

I? This time she didn't give the dark voice time to answer her.

"Open your eyes, Soona. Everything's alright now." She looked over her shoulder to where Soona sat with one large hand cupping Hal's head and the other over her eyes like a child playing hide-and-seek.

"It's okay, you can look now."

Soona slid the hand away from her face and her gaze rolled from Paige to the window. It might have been a trick of the light, but she thought she saw tears on the woman's cheeks. *I just killed her mother.* No, she corrected herself. *I just saved my family.*

Up ahead the road T-junctioned. Slumped to the right, using the door to keep herself propped up, Paige turned left and drove in what she prayed was the direction of the roadhouse.

Chapter Twenty-Six

Norrison Littleman woke with a gasp, the bedsheet clenched in a grey bunch between his hands. Next to him his wife, Tilda, snored softly. The dream, so vivid only seconds ago, slipped out of his grasp. One thing remained, the gunshot. He'd been sitting in a swing; that he was sure of. Flying back and forth. He frowned in the dark. He tried to recall the details of his trip through the air, but all he could clearly recall was a crack. Distant, but clearly a gunshot.

He sat up wincing and slid his legs over the side of the bed, careful not to wake his slumbering lady. Yesterday had been delivery day and that meant lifting and carrying crates until his back howled like a banshee with its tail on fire. Tilda, a small delicate creature, fell into bed exhausted at nine o'clock.

"Keep your hands to yourself tonight, Norrie. After the lifting and carrying I've done today, I'd turn down Clint Eastwood even if he were holding a beer in one hand and a slab of chocolate in the other." With that, Tilda rolled onto her side and within minutes her breathing evened out into soft snores.

Norrie didn't say it, but he had no intention of starting anything that his aching back wouldn't let him finish. Besides, at sixty-three he wasn't the stud he used to be. A small truth that Tilda didn't need to know. He was more than happy for her to fall asleep thinking her stallion of a husband was going without for her benefit.

He exited the bedroom and closed the door with a soft click and padded past the kitchen. When he reached the back door, he flicked on the outside lights. The door, a faded wooden frame with a sagging screen was unlocked. He grabbed his smokes off the windowsill, fleetingly wondering if they were the reason his libido was hitting the bricks, and pushed the door open.

The back of the Million Miles roadhouse consisted of a scrubby patch of weeds and dry grass with a three-metre-wide stretch of paving abutting the exit. Norrie lit a smoke and plopped down into the white plastic chair that made up one fourth of the mismatched setting decorating the spot Tilda liked to call – with no hint of humour – their alfresco area.

With the dream that woke him still skirting the edges of his mind, Norrie puffed his smoke and listened to the crickets sing. *A swing of all things*, he thought with a small chuckle. *There's barely a red hair left on my head and I'm dreaming about riding on a swing*. He decided to tell Tilda about the dream in the morning, she'd get a real kick out of it.

He finished his smoke and considered going back to bed, then dismissed the idea in favour of a cup of hot chocolate. Sleep was harder to come by in his old age. *Something chocolatey and warm might just be the ticket,* he thought and headed back inside.

Ten minutes later, Norrie sat back enjoying the comfort of the alfresco area. He sniffed the steaming chocolate and blew absently into the cup. With the night air pleasantly fresh, almost chilly, the hot cup felt comforting in his hands. His mind kept returning to the dream. The swinging was one thing; funny, yet understandable. But the gunshot bugged him. Maybe he was turning into an old fusspot, but he couldn't get it out of his mind. The sound, like a whip crack in a tunnel had been so real. *Maybe I'm having a series of minor strokes,* he thought and shuddered at the idea.

Without thinking, he put the cup on the pavers next to his chair and fumbled another smoke out of his packet. Before he had time to flick on the lighter, the unmistakable crunch of tyres on the forecourt stilled his hand.

Norrie cocked his head to the left and waited for the thud of car doors. He hadn't bothered to check the time on the kitchen clock, but felt sure it was late; after midnight. Whoever owned the vehicle sitting in front of the roadhouse was either lost or looking for trouble. When no sound came but the faint hum of an engine, he stood and glanced towards the back door. His heart kicked up a notch.

He kept a cricket bat under the counter in the shop. A stained Gray-Nicolls Strokemaster with red and black tape around the grip. He thought of going inside and retrieving it. He'd run the Million Miles for fifteen years, him and Tilda; he wouldn't need lights to find his way through the kitchen and into the shop. He raked his hand over his sparsely covered pate and liked his lips. *I'll ring the cops while I'm at it,* he thought and nodded his head.

The roadhouse was isolated. The nearest neighbour twenty minutes away, the loopy old Sheila at Mable house. *Not that the Hatcher woman could be described as neighbourly.* But that was fine with him, isolated meant peaceful. But in the dark of night, it could mean vulnerable. The last thing Norrie wanted was a punch-up with a gang of yobbos hyped up on meth or whatever kids these days liked shoving up their noses. *Or down their lungs,* he thought with disgust.

He put his hand on the screen door and wasn't surprised to see his fingers trembling. *If there's assholes trying to rob us, this is going to get ugly*, he thought with more than a little trepidation. He pulled the door open slowly to silence the squeal of the hinges. *I've gotta get some WD40 on those*, he thought, grimacing at how loud the door sounded when everything else was still. He'd just put one bare foot in the house when a car horn, as load as a scream, filled the night.

His already jangled nerves got the better of him. The door slipped out of his hand and snapped shut with a thump. He stepped back and hit the chair he'd been sitting in, knocking it and the cup of hot chocolate over.

"Shit," he yelped as hot liquid splashed his ankle.

The horn continued to blast, desperate and urgent. All thoughts of robbery left his mind and for the first time since he heard the car, Norrie wondered if someone might be in trouble. He jogged around the back of the building ignoring the prickles and stones under his bare feet. When he reached the forecourt he stopped, out of breath from the short dash.

An orange four-wheel-drive sat to the left of the roadhouse, horn howling and bathed in moonlight. Still breathing hard, Norrie took a tentative step towards the vehicle. The windows were tinted, but he thought he saw movement in the back seat.

"What's going on?" Tilda's voice at his shoulder made him jump.

"Jesus, Til. You nearly stopped my heart." Norrie looked back at the four-wheel-drive. The front grille looked dented and there were brownish looking smears across the bonnet. "I think someone's hurt. You go back inside and call the cops. I'm going to take a closer look."

Tilda grabbed his shoulder, her small fingers dug into the skin above his collar bone. "I don't like this. I think we should wait inside and let the police sort it out."

Norrie disengaged his wife's grip and took a step forward. "I don't like it any more than you, but if

198

someone's hurt, I'm not sitting inside with my thumb up my ass until the cops get here. Now go inside."

Normally, giving Tilda an order would incur not only a tongue lashing but possibly a few days' silent treatment. Instead of arguing, she pressed the handle of the cricket bat into Norrie's hand.

"Take this with you. I'll wait until I know you're safe, then I'll go inside."

Norrie swallowed and nodded. Tilda looked like a tiny frightened bird draped in a long blue nightdress. He had the urge to wrap his arms around her and kiss the top of her head. *I'm too old to be playing the hero*, he thought, and walked towards the car. He noticed the right headlight had a jagged crack running through it.

When he reached the driver's door, he made out a shape hunched against the wheel. *If it's a drunk, I'll brain him*. Norrie reached for the handle. He pulled the door open with his right hand and raised the bat with his left. When the interior light came on, he let out a gasp and the bat slid out of his sweaty hand.

"Holy God!"

"What is it? Is someone hurt?" Tilda's voice came almost as a scream over the blare of the horn.

"Call an ambulance!" Norrie looked back at his wife. "Now!"

Chapter Twenty-Seven

Something damp touched the side of Paige's face. She flinched and raised her hand to ward off the attack.

"It's alright, love. You're safe." A woman's voice.

Paige blinked. Her eyes moved slowly, as if weighed down with mud. She tried moving her head, but a whooshing sound filled her ears and a razor wire of pain pierced her groin.

"Don't try to move. Just keep still and the ambulance will be here soon." The woman's voice had a gentle comforting quality.

Paige managed to open her eyes. The light, soft and yellow, brought details into focus. The car door, a woman's face – small and dominated by watery blue eyes.

"Amb … Ambulance?" Her tongue stuck to the roof of her mouth.

"Yes." The woman lifted a white cloth and dabbed Paige's forehead. "You're at the Million Miles Roadhouse. The air ambulance is on its way. But you mustn't move."

The roadhouse, Wade was right, Paige thought. *It wasn't far.* The panic stabbed at her. "Hal? Where's Hal? He needs …"

"It's okay. He's still in the back of the car. They'll look after him too. I promise."

Paige let out a shuddering breath. She'd made it. They were safe.

"What's your name, love?" The question pulled Paige back to the present.

She focused her eyes on the face that hovered next to her. She blinked and the face changed. The watery blue eyes were replaced by bulging grey shark eyes. Paige shrieked and tried to pull away.

"It's alright. No one's going to hurt you." The woman's voice broke through Paige's panic and once more the kindly blue eyes looked at her.

"I'm ... I'm Paige." Her name came out in a sigh of air.

"Okay, Paige. I'm Tilda and that Yobbo behind me is Norrie." Tilda gestured over her shoulder.

For the first time since opening her eyes, Paige noticed the bald man standing behind the woman. He nodded to her, but didn't speak. Tilda raised her hand to dab at Paige's forehead. With strength she didn't know she had, Paige grabbed the woman's hand. Tilda let out a gasp of surprise but didn't pull away.

"Is my baby okay?" Paige squeezed Tilda's wrist. "It's not too late is it? They'll save the baby, won't they?" The words came out around sobs and her eyes blurred with tears. Her rational mind told her the kindly woman next to her couldn't answer those questions, but she wanted, no, *needed* Tilda to tell her the baby was okay.

Tilda patted Paige's hand, the one wrapped around the woman's small wrist. "I promise they'll do everything they can to save your baby. But you have to help by staying calm and keeping still. Okay?"

Paige worked her mouth trying to answer but a deafening roar pierced the night and blocked out her thoughts. From the back of the car came a now familiar chant. "Don't touch. Don't touch."

"It's okay, sweetheart," Paige whispered. Don't be afraid. It's the ambulance." Paige squeezed her eyes shut and let darkness swallow her.

* * *

She became aware of movement. Her body seemed to be vibrating. Paige opened her eyes and took in her surroundings. Not all at once but in snatches of images. Grey metal above her head. A man leaning over her. Hal lying on a stretcher, his eyes closed, straps encircling his body.

"Hal?" Her voice sounded weak, swamped by the noise overhead.

"He's hanging in there." The man above her looked young. A teenager. *No*, Paige told herself he's not a teenager, he's a medic.

"Paige," he spoke again. "I'm Brandon. I'm a medic. Can you tell me how many weeks you are?"

"Its ... I'm...almost thirty weeks."

He nodded. "Okay. Good. Have you had any contractions?"

Paige nodded. "Is my baby okay?"

Brandon's face flushed with colour. "We're going to do everything we can. We're taking you to Bunbury hospital where you'll most likely be taken down to theatre." He paused and she felt him touch her shoulder. "Just hang on, Paige. We'll do everything we can.

Yes, Tilda promised. Brandon's voice drifted over her. He was asking her something, but his words made no sense. She looked over at Hal and then let her eyes close, grateful for the darkness.

Chapter Twenty-Eight

Paige lifted a slat on the blinds and leaned her head closer to the window. The angle allowed her a clear view of the mailbox and driveway where Hal was making his way towards the house. He leaned to the right and wedged the crutch under his arm. Then, in a practiced movement, he pulled a bundle of envelopes out of his teeth and stuffed them down the front of his shorts. He leaned his considerably thinner frame on the left crutch and lifted his prosthetic leg. With his head down, he limped his way to the front door. His determination never ceased to amaze her.

Paige pulled back from the window and walked into the kitchen. She returned to the table and the blank computer screen in time to hear Hal clomp into the house. In the four months since what Paige now thought of as *the incident* – she refused to use the woman's name and would only discuss the four days they spent at Mable House when pushed by Hal or the police – Hal had been through three surgeries. The first took place on the night they escaped.

Her recollection remained clear. *Too* clear. She remembered everything in almost minute detail: The look on Hatcher's face as she was sucked under the car; the agonising tearing in her swollen belly when the gun fired. The images in her head so vivid, she could even see the little specks of dust on the windshield and hear the cracking sound that came when the body rolled beneath the wheels. Sometimes, mostly at night, but even when she was thinking about other things like what to cook for dinner, that cracking sound would pop into her head. Other times, she'd think she felt the baby kick, and her hand would go to her now flat stomach.

"Some mail." Hal put the envelopes on the table. "How's the resume going?"

Paige scratched her forehead and picked up the envelopes. "Not very well."

She felt Hal's fingers brush the back of her neck. "There's no rush."

"Hal," she hesitated. "I don't think I can go back to teaching."

Hal manoeuvred himself into the chair directly across from her and leaned his crutches against the table. There were greys sprinkled throughout his messy brown hair and a network of fine lines beneath his eyes. *When did that happen?* Paige wondered. She'd noticed similar changes in the mirror; only the tight lines around her mouth made her look hard in a way Hal's face never could.

He waited for her to continue, but how could she explain when she didn't really understand herself? All she knew was that she couldn't stand up in front of all those innocent young faces and pretend the world was a safe and happy place. She couldn't be the one with all the answers. Not anymore. Not after what she'd done.

"I just don't want to do it anymore." She couldn't bear the look of sadness in his eyes. Eyes that had lost some of their sparkle. "I'm thinking I could go back to retail. I used to work in a boutique when I was at uni. I was good at it." She clenched her hands in her lap to keep from touching her stomach. "What do you think?"

"I think you're good at helping people. You'd be wasted in a dress shop, but if it's what you want then give it a try." He rubbed his left thigh and frowned.

When the medics had rushed Hal into surgery, his left leg was badly infected. The stump contained fragments of splintered bone and the infection had spread from the wound to the tissue surrounding his knee. Doctors made the decision to amputate at mid-thigh, a decision that if delayed would have most likely cost him his life.

His right leg also needed surgery. The bone was displaced and had been left untreated and incorrectly splinted for four days, making it impossible for surgeons to set the leg without inserting a rod and several bolts to hold the bones in place. Since that night, he'd undergone two more surgeries. One to remove the temporary rod and replace it with smaller plates and screws, and another revision surgery on his stump to extend its length using a skin graft.

"How's the pain?"

"Not bad." He reached for his crutches. "Let's go out for dinner tonight."

"Um." Paige felt caught off balance by the suggestion. The thought of getting dressed up and going out in public was by equal measures exhausting and terrifying. Not that she could articulate what frightened her about going to a restaurant with her husband.

Hal waited for her response. She could see worry building in his eyes. "Yes, okay. That sounds good."

His face brightened. "One of the perks of having one leg is the disabled parking, which means no driving around looking for a spot."

Paige let out a gasp that turned into a laugh. Her first genuine laugh in four months. She was so surprised by Hal's comment *and* her response, that she slapped her hand over her mouth.

Hal responded with a devilish smile. "Paige, I can't believe you're laughing at the disabled," he said in mock disapproval.

She felt another fit of laughter bubble up in her throat. This time she didn't try to hide it. She dropped her hand into her lap and really let lose. And just like that, the two of them were chuckling away like school children. They were Paige and Hal again. In love with their whole lives ahead of them. The moment was wonderful, but tantalisingly short.

Paige found herself remembering the day in the car when Hal put his hand on her belly and felt their son kick. The way he'd looked at her over his sunglasses. The blissful feeling of contentment she'd felt. She'd expected that feeling to last forever. Was this how life would be now? Snatches of happiness that were nothing more than cruel reminders of how things could have been.

"What's wrong, honey?"

Paige realised she'd stopped laughing, and Hal stared at her with all too familiar concern.

"Nothing. I … Nothing." Paige stood up and moved over to the sink so she wouldn't have to look at him.

"You were thinking about the baby. About Jacob, weren't you?" His voice soft, almost a whisper.

At the mention of her son's name, Paige felt her body sag. She didn't want to ruin the brief moment they'd just shared. Hal was trying so hard to put everything back together. He'd never shown anger or resentment over what had been done to him. Even the pain didn't slow him down. Compared to him, Paige felt weak and selfish.

"I'm sorry, Hal. I'm trying." She bit her lip and tried to keep her shoulders from curling in like a crumpled leaf.

She heard Hal stand and take up his crutches. He would come to her now and give her comfort. She would take it and sob in his arms, all the while hating herself for not being strong enough to ease his grief. Jacob was his son too.

Paige woke with a start. Her hair clung to her face and neck in sweaty strings. The room was dark and for a moment she thought she was back in Mable House. Hal stirred next to her and mumbled something. It sounded like *monster eyes*, but she couldn't be sure.

She sat up and put her hand on Hal's shoulder. Her touch always seemed to calm him, as if it grounded him somehow. His breathing evened out and soon his shoulders relaxed. Paige waited another minute to make sure he was sleeping peacefully and slipped out of bed. The chill of the night air leaked into her bones, she shivered and grabbed her cardigan from the end of the bed. Wrapping it around her shoulders, she left the room as silently as possible.

The clock on the microwave showed 4:00 am. Paige padded across the kitchen and slid the back door open. Sitting on the back porch watching the stars had become her nightly ritual. Under the vastness of the sky her problems seemed smaller and the world clearer. Maybe it was the stars and the way they gleamed that turned her thoughts to Jacob. Whatever the reason, she found herself imagining the chubby-cheeked infant he would have been at four months.

It occurred to her that her body woke every night because this is what she would have been doing if her child had lived. She'd be holding him, feeding him. Paige slipped her arms through the sleeves of her cardigan and hugged herself. The night they'd escaped from Mable House, medics rushed her to the women's hospital where she underwent an emergency caesarean section. Amidst all the craziness, her memories of the moments leading up to the surgery were burned into her mind.

Flown by helicopter to the city, she remembered a young man, he said his name was Brandon, leaning over her. There was kindness in his tanned, young face. He asked her questions. His voice gentle and difficult to hear over the sound of the helicopter's whirring blades. Paige remembered asking if the baby was going to be okay. A silly question really. How could the young man know what was happening inside her?

In the end, all her questions were answered by the doctor that delivered her little boy. Dr Carson explained that she'd gone into early labour and then, most likely due to trauma, the labour had stopped.

"I'm very sorry, Mrs. Loche but your baby didn't survive." Paige flinched as if the words spoken that night were just whispered in her ear.

She stood. A crescent moon offered little in the way of light. Summer nights were usually much warmer. She should go back to bed where she could fold herself against Hal and soak in his warmth. But instead of going inside she stayed on the back porch watching the moon. The grief that held her, woke her each night and brought her outside was almost addictive. Some nights she wanted to give in to it and let herself drown in its depths. Nights like this were gardens where despair flourished.

"Paige?" Hal's voice startled her. Her face felt damp. She realised she'd been crying.

"Did I wake you?"

"No," he said, and used his crutches to manoeuvre himself out onto the porch. Without his prosthetic leg, it was difficult for him to balance. Paige immediately felt guilty for bringing him out in the cold.

"It's okay. I'm just coming in. Let's go back to bed." She knew he couldn't see her tears in the dark, but the tremor in her voice betrayed her.

Hal didn't move. "Let's go inside and have some hot chocolate. I think we should talk." There was worry in his voice, and something else. "There's something I want to show you."

* * *

Paige curled her hands around the steaming cup and let the heat soak into her arms. She noticed the clock over the table – nearly 4:30 am. Hal sat across from her staring at his hot chocolate. He seemed to be in a strangely un-talkative mood for a man who wanted to talk. The silence made Paige nervous. She felt the need to fill it with noise.

"What did you want to show me?" She took a sip from her mug. "I'm starting to get a weird feeling sitting here in silence." She laughed; it was a nervous sound.

Hal let out a long sigh and rubbed his hand across his chin. "I know you get up every night and sit outside. I also know you're thinking about what happened and ..." he paused, still staring at his drink. "I know you're thinking about Jacob."

"I'm just trying to ..."

Hal held up his hand. "I'm not attacking you, honey. It's natural to be grieving, but it's more than that. It's like you're slipping away. I feel like I'm losing you in small pieces." He looked up and what Paige saw in his eyes stabbed at her heart. "I can't lose anything else, Paige."

She wanted to give him assurances, make promises, but couldn't bring herself to lie to him. "I'm trying, Hal." It didn't sound like much.

He nodded and took her hand. "What happened to us was ..."

Paige stood. "I don't want to talk about what happened. I'm tired, Hal." She tried to walk away, but he held her hand in both of his, refusing to let go. "Hal, please. We can do this another time."

"No." The anger in his voice surprised her and she sat back down. "We're doing it now. If we don't talk about it, it'll eat up everything we've got until we're strangers."

Paige dropped her free hand in her lap and nodded. Exhaustion washed over her. "Okay."

Hal's grip softened, but he didn't release her. "I know you're trying to come to terms with ..." he swallowed. "With losing Jacob. So am I." The last three words were a whisper that brought tears to Paige's eyes. "It's going to take us both time to find a way back."

Paige nodded, eyes fixed on her lap. She hated the pain in his voice when he spoke of Jacob. The old Paige would've put her arms around him, tried to ease that pain. But there was a hard nugget of ice in the pit of her stomach. It began to form when she drove the car over that witch. Maybe the crack she'd heard that night came from inside her as much as it did from the woman's body.

"I know you're struggling with what you did."

Paige's head shot up. It was in his eyes, he knew. *How could he know? He was unconscious.* Paige told the police that Lizzy ran out in front of the car and she didn't have time to stop. No one knew what she'd done, except Soona. *I told her to close her eyes while I killed her mother.* Paige tried to work her mouth, not sure what she wanted to say. She couldn't lie to him. She'd done so much already, but couldn't bring herself to deny what they both knew.

"How … how do you …?" Unsure how to finish the question, she let the words hang.

Hal turned her hand over and opened her palm. Then lifted it to his mouth and kissed the soft pad below her thumb. "I heard you tell Soona to close her eyes. I knew what you were doing. I've known all along." His tone carried no accusation or anger.

"Why didn't you say anything?" Part of her felt ugly and exposed, but also relieved. He *knew.* He wasn't turning away from her in disgust. Why had she ever thought he would?

"You didn't want to talk about what happened at Mable House. And I … I'm not as strong as you." He paused and deep creases gathered on his forehead. "You did what I couldn't. You saved me. You saved *us.* You did nothing wrong."

"I wish I could believe that, Hal. But I could have driven around her. She couldn't have stopped me. I killed her because I wanted to." The words were out and with them came a rush of relief. She felt as though she'd been underwater holding her breath, and after months of struggling to find the surface, she broke free. "I wanted her dead for what she did to you. I knew … knew the baby was dead. I tried to pretend I didn't, but … I could feel it." A gasp that came from deep in her chest burst out.

She pulled her hand free from Hal's grip and wrapped her arms around herself. "I knew. She killed our baby. She butchered you." Tears ran down her cheeks and her voice trembled and cracked with each word. "Oh God, Hal, I enjoyed killing her." She swiped her arm across her face, smearing tears on the sleeve of her cardigan.

Hal stood awkwardly, leaning on the table. He grabbed her shoulder and pulled her up into his arms. "Paige, you need to listen to me and really hear what I'm saying." His voice was steady and unwavering. He pushed her back and held her away from him. "Please?"

The gravity in his tone broke through the tidal wave of guilt. She managed to gather herself enough to nod.

"Okay. Now sit. I'm going to get us something stronger to drink."

Paige did as he instructed and watched her husband clomp around the kitchen. He took two glasses out of the cupboard above the sink, then a bottle of whisky from the top shelf of the pantry. He poured a couple of fingers of the amber liquid into each glass, before bringing the drinks to the table one at a time. Paige didn't get up or offer any help. It had become their unspoken agreement, she only helped him when he asked.

She took a sip of the whiskey and grimaced. "Urgh. This stuff's awful."

A smile drifted across his face and then disappeared. "That place, Mable House. There was something very wrong about it." He took a swig of his drink. "I could feel it working on me. I wanted to kill her, and not just to make her stop, but because I knew I'd enjoy it."

Paige took another sip of her drink, this time the burning sensation in her throat felt good. It made it easier to listen to the words coming from Hal's mouth.

"I don't know if whatever it was came from her." He paused and took another sip. "Maybe it was already there before she was born. Maybe it came from all the suffering of those soldiers and the young women that had their babies taken away." He shrugged. "I don't know, but there *was* something. It kept working on me. I could feel it." His eyes were burning into her. "Am I crazy?"

Paige shook her head. She'd felt it too. That day in Lizzy's bedroom, when she was searching for the keys and found the gun. She'd felt it. Something black and vicious lurking in those rooms. A force that fed off the misery and fear in that building. Urging her on.

"You're not crazy. I felt it too, I don't know how to explain it." Her eyes widened. "I gave in to it." She tipped her glass and drained the last few drops. "What does that make me?"

"It makes you a good person pushed to the limit. You did what you had to, to protect your family. Because we were touched by evil, doesn't make us evil."

"I want to believe that, Hal. I really do, but …"

"Let me show you something." He put his glass down and picked up the stack of mail he'd brought in that day. *Or was it yesterday?* Paige noticed the weak streak of light behind him, just outside the window, and realised it was nearly morning.

"I think you should look at this," he said, holding up an envelope. "I was going to show it to you last night, but you seemed so far away at dinner." His voice trailed off and he held the letter out.

It was addressed to both of them, handwritten. *Handwritten envelopes are so rare nowadays*, Paige thought absently and took it from him. She ran her finger along the top edge, torn where Hal had opened it. Curious, she slid out a handwritten letter and a drawing. The drawing took her by surprise. She drew in a quick breath and looked up at Hal. He nodded for her to read the letter.

Dear Mr and Mrs. Loche,

My name is Susanne, I'm a care assistant at Grange Gardens. I hope you don't mind me contacting you, but Soona wanted me to send you this drawing.

When she first came to us, she was almost non-verbal but now she's a bit of a chatterbox. As you can see by the drawing, she's learning to write and is coming on in leaps and bounds.

Yours were the only contact details in her file and she often talks about Paige. She calls you "my Paige." Anyway, enjoy the drawing and if you would like to write to Soona, I know she'd be delighted to receive a letter.

Thanks

Susanne Vernette

Paige wiped a tear from under her eye and put the letter on the table. She picked up the drawing. A stick figure in blue overalls holding hands with another stick figure in a grey dress. They both held flowers in their free hands. The figure in the grey dress had yellow hair jutting straight up and big blue circles for eyes. Above them sat an orange sun and what looked like a flying chicken. At the bottom of the page in large childish writing sat three words: *Soona and Paige*. The S was back to front and the e on the end of Paige drooped down at a drunken angle.

She touched her finger to the waxy figures in the drawing and couldn't help smiling.

"You got her out of there. You didn't give in to evil, you protected innocence against it. I heard you. You told Soona to *close* her eyes. You were still trying to keep her from seeing the ugly stuff." He leaned forward. "And you did. You have to hang on to that."

"I will." She put the drawing on the table and took his face in her hands. "I'll hang on." She kissed him and then they went outside and watched the weak streaks of light turn into a glorious sunrise. There were still dark days ahead, but maybe there was light too. All she had to do was find it.

If you enjoyed this book, please let others know by leaving a quick review on Amazon. Also, if you spot anything untoward in the paperback, get in touch. We strive for the best quality and appreciate reader feedback.

editor@thebookfolks.com

www.thebookfolks.com

RETRIBUTION RIDGE

Milly thinks that her sister's invitation to go hiking in the Outback is a chance to heal old wounds. Think again Milly. But what greets them in the wilderness is far more than the humiliation her sister had prepared. It is a confrontation with her worst fears.

UNWELCOME GUESTS

Caitlin seeks to build bridges with her husband after the loss of their baby. Unfortunately, their holiday getaway is not what it seems when they find a man held hostage in the cellar. When the house owner turns up, armed and dangerous, Caitlin will have to quickly decide whom she should trust.

FORGOTTEN CRIMES

A reunion with her friend Rhetty, triggers a series of
flashbacks for Gloria of events that occurred four years
previously. Rhetty encourages Gloria to revisit the site
where a woman died to understand the strange memories.
But doing so will put her in danger and force her to
confront an awful episode in her past.

CRUELTY'S DAUGHTER

Mina's father was a brute and a thug. She got over him.
Now another man wants to fill his shoes. Can Mina
overcome the past and protect herself? 'Cruelty's
Daughter' is about a woman who tackles her demons and
takes it upon herself to turn the tables on a violent man.

VENGEANCE BLIND

Of poor eyesight and confined to a wheelchair, a successful author is alone in her house. She begins to hear strange noises, but is relieved when a care assistant arrives. However, her problems are only just beginning as she is left to the mercy of someone with a grudge to bear.

THE WOMAN BEHIND HER

When Jackie Winter inherits her aunt's house, she makes a chilling discovery. Worse, she finds that she is being watched. When someone is murdered nearby, she finds herself in the frame. Can she join up the dots and prove her innocence?

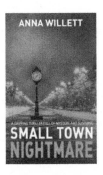

SMALL TOWN NIGHTMARE

Lucy's brother is the only close family she has. So, when he goes missing, she begins to panic. She heads out to a rural backwater, Night Town, his last known location, but when she investigates deeper the locals don't respond kindly. What lengths will the townsfolk go to protect their secrets? And how far will she go to protect her kin?

COLD VALLEY NIGHTMARE

Investigative journalist, Lucy, agrees to help look for a child who has gone missing in suspicious circumstances. But in so doing she will have to confront her own feelings of loss and abandonment. When she uncovers a dangerous criminal network, she'll have to draw on all her resolve to escape and see her mission through.

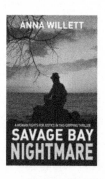

SAVAGE BAY NIGHTMARE

When journalist Lucy Hush's brother is accused of
murder, she goes on a desperate search for the truth. But
her inquiries are unwelcome and it's not long before she
stirs up a vipers' nest full of subterfuge and deceit. Can she
get justice for her brother, or will she become another
victim?

*All of these books are available free with Kindle Unlimited and in
paperback from Amazon*

Made in the USA
Monee, IL
21 November 2022

18264594R00135